Unarm

Hooked #5

Charity Parkerson

--Warning: This book is intended for readers over the age of 18.

Copyright © 2017 Charity Parkerson

Editor: Hercules Editing and Consultants

Photographer: Strangeland Photography
(http://strangelandphotography.com/)

Introduction

All it took was one night with Jace, and Tyler was hooked. Too bad it took less than one night for him to ruin any chance of being with Jace.

Twenty years of working with endangered and exploited children has left Tyler tired and jaded. Even though he's solved hundreds of cases, saving children all over the country, the countless he couldn't save haunt his dreams. He's yet to meet a man who can tolerate his dark moods for long. That is, until he meets Jace.

Jace has spent his life used and mistreated by men. Even though he keeps up a strong face, he's exhausted and his self-esteem is non-existent. Something about Tyler is different from the rest. For Jace, Tyler checks every box. However, the instant he gives Tyler a chance, the man crushes him, proving he's exactly like every other man Jace has ever met.

Tyler hates that he's hurt Jace. Although he immediately regrets his actions, he also doesn't know how to build a real relationship when he doesn't think he has anything to offer. How can two men who've never known love recognize it, even when it's staring them in the face? They'd better figure things out quick, because their relationship is heating up fast. Neither man wants to get burned, and there's already one person who can't wait to destroy what they have.

Chapter 1

They'd met once before, when Jace had been dating Jimmy. That didn't explain why Tyler was on Jace's doorstep now or why he was staring at Jace the way he was.

"Hey, Tyler. What brings you by?"

Tyler shook his head as if shaking off a trance. "I'm looking for Jimmy." His words came out stilted, as if his mind was in one place while his mouth was in another. "I've checked both bars, and he wasn't at either."

"Did you check his house?"

Tyler blinked. "The idea never crossed my mind. He's never home."

Jace pasted on his kindest smile. If anyone understood the craziness of caring about Jimmy, it was Jace. "From what I understand, he rarely leaves the house, other than to go to the gym, since Eli moved in."

A deep line appeared between Tyler's eyes. "Who the hell is Eli?"

Jace shifted—uncomfortable. "Jimmy's boyfriend." It took every ounce of Jace's willpower not to stress the word "boy." He wasn't bitter—much. He also didn't miss Jimmy. It was more about his stinging pride than anything. If anything, Tyler looked more confused by Jace's answer.

"When did that happen? I thought the two of you were still dating. That's why I stopped by here."

Jace shook his head. "Not for a while now."

Tyler didn't respond. His gaze continued to move over Jace's face, as if

6

confused by Jace. The longer Tyler stared, the more uncomfortable Jace became. He caught himself brushing his cheek, wondering if he had something on his face. Makeup smeared his fingers. Heat filled his cheeks.

"Oh, I forgot. My nephew is in the running for an internship with Rylan Santos, the makeup artist for the stars. He's friends with countless women who'll let him use them as test subjccts, but other than himself, I'm the only man willing to be his guinea pig. It completely slipped my mind he'd been experimenting on me earlier. No wonder you've been staring at me like that. You must think I'm crazy."

"How was I staring at you?" Tyler asked without missing a beat.

A smile pulled at the corners of Jace's mouth. "Like you don't know what to do with me."

Tyler shook his head. When he responded, his voice deepened. "That's not how I was staring at you, and I definitely wasn't thinking you're crazy."

It was the way Tyler said each word. Jace's mouth went dry. Being with Jimmy had wrecked Jace's self-confidence. He shouldn't have let it happen, but damn. It had really fucked with his head the way Jimmy had obviously been completely uninterested in anything sexual with Jace. He wasn't sure why Jimmy had wanted to be with him at all. The man had kissed him several times, as if he wanted more, but always stopped short of sealing the deal. At first, he'd thought Jimmy was being respectful. Then he'd thought Jimmy's horrible past held him back. Eli had come along and it couldn't have been more obvious Jimmy wasn't having a single problem getting it up for that boy. Jace shoved his bitter thoughts aside. He needed to stop dwelling on it, which would be a lot easier if he didn't feel so damn lacking. Jace hated not liking himself. Now Tyler had butterflies stirring in Jace's stomach.

"Damn," Jace said, breathlessly, before he could call it back. "I'm dying to know what you were thinking."

Tyler's features transformed, leaving Jace feeling flattened. A polite smile touched the man's sexy lips. It couldn't have been more apparent Tyler was shutting Jace down. "Sorry for bothering you. Thanks for the info. I'll check Jimmy's house."

Jace felt his face harden into a fake smile. "Sure thing." Even to Jace's ears, he sounded overly bright. "Good luck with your search."

Tyler nodded and turned to leave. Before Tyler made it three steps, he reversed course, coming to stand toe to toe with Jace. "I wasn't staring at you like I don't know what to do with you. The opposite, in fact. I know exactly what I'd like to do with you. Also, I can't leave without saying, your nephew totally deserves that internship. You have the most beautiful eyes I've ever seen, and he did an amazing job of making them stand out." His heated gaze swept down Jace's body before he added, "Not that I'm saying they're your best feature. Really, the whole thing is... damn."

Heat exploded through Jace's face.

Tyler's mouth lifted in one corner. "Have dinner with me."

"You're looking for Jimmy, remember?" Jace said, hating his need to remind Tyler of his errand. He hadn't been so tempted in a long time.

"I'll find him tomorrow. It's late. Like dinner time late. We should eat."

He was torn. This man had raised Jimmy from fourteen. Even though there wasn't a huge age difference between Tyler and Jimmy, he was like the man's dad. Nonetheless, Jace wanted to go. It wasn't as if he'd ever been serious with Jimmy, and Tyler didn't seem to mind.

"Let me wash this stuff off and change clothes."

Tyler's gaze raked Jace's body once more, making Jace burn. "Or you could go as you are; whatever you're comfortable with."

"I'll change," Jace repeated, waving Tyler inside.

*

As Tyler crossed the threshold of Jace's house, he questioned his sanity. He'd started out the evening determined to find Jimmy. Now a different hunt filled his head. Months ago, when he'd met Jace, Tyler would've had to have been blind not to notice how incredibly sexy Jace was, but that was as far as his thoughts had gone on the matter.

When Jace answered the door tonight, Tyler's mind had blanked. With his eyes coated in eyeliner and a light tint to his sexy lips, Jace had Tyler's mind going one place. Jace was the most beautiful man Tyler had ever seen. Tyler had never wanted to touch anyone as badly—just to see if he was real. The offer for dinner was an impulsive one. Tyler wouldn't take it back.

"Can I get you something to drink while you wait?"

"I'm good," Tyler said, taking a seat on

the plush leather sofa. "Do what you need to. I'm a patient guy." He was, but not when it came to sexy men. Tyler's dick was already stirring at the thought of Jace taking off his clothes, even if it was only long enough for Jace to change into something else.

"I'll hurry." The husky note to Jace's voice had Tyler wondering if he knew Tyler was half turned on already.

Once Jace disappeared down the hall, Tyler swept his gaze over the room to give himself something to do other than picturing a nude Jace close by. The walls were an off-white—like countless other homes, but Jace's house had extra touches, letting Tyler know the man had invested a ton of money in the place. Arched doorways were the first giveaway. Plus, the place just smelled expensive— like polished wood and something flowery. Even the curtains looked custom made.

By the time Tyler spotted Jace making his way back down the hall, he'd convinced himself the dude was way out of Tyler's league.

Then Jace stepped into view, and Tyler no longer cared. It was cool outside for late September, and Jace dressed the part. His dark jeans cupped the man's ass to perfection. However, it was the long-sleeve henley straining against Jace's biceps that had Tyler's mouth watering. The man's body was beyond amazing. Tyler was on his feet and moving closer before he realized it—as if he was drawn in by Jace's sexiness like a magnet.

"What do you do for a living?" Tyler had no clue where the conversational-type question came from, considering he was thinking of ripping Jace's clothes off and stalking the man like he was prey.

Jace's smile was everything. "I'm a dental hygienist at Oak Ridge Dental."

"I have to say I've never had a dentist who looks like you. It must be hard work pulling teeth to get muscles like these," he said, using their discussion as an excuse to touch Jace's arms. Fuck. They felt as good as they looked.

A sexy-sounding chuckle left Jace and caressed Tyler's ears. "I don't pull teeth. That's a dentist. I'm a hygienist. I clean teeth. The muscle is from fighting."

That brought Tyler up short before realization set in. He snapped his fingers. "That's right. You do the MMA thing with Jimmy?"

Jace's nose curled as they headed for the door. Jesus. Tyler didn't know if he'd survive the upcoming meal. He wanted to stay here and savor Jace instead.

"Actually, I'm in a different weight class than Jimmy, but I get what you're saying. We fight for the same gym—Smith Brothers. It's just a hobby for me. I like the

15

release of pent-up energy."

Tyler's stomach growled. He laughed at the sound. "Sorry. I'm starving." He really was, but not for food. It had been too long since Tyler lost himself in another man's body. He was certain he'd never indulged in anyone half as sexy as Jace.

* * *

Tyler was amazing. Every smile, word, and heated glance had Jace blushing. Their food disappeared with no real thought. Jace's focus remained locked on Tyler the entire meal. There was never a pause in the conversation because Jace wanted to know all the details of Tyler's life. He'd asked so many questions, it was a miracle Tyler managed to sneak in a single bite.

With his gaze locked on Jace's face, Tyler set his elbows on the table and leaned closer. "Your skin is flushed. It makes your sexy eyes stand out even more. I imagine if I kissed you, you'd look the same way afterward."

"It's the excitement," Jace admitted without shame.

"From being with me?" Tyler asked, sounding doubtful. "You should be bored off your ass. I'm the least exciting person I know."

"It's the way you're staring at me—like you're imagining all the naughty things you could do. I haven't felt desired in a long time." Horror choked Jace. "I don't know why I just said that."

Tyler shrugged, taking the sting from Jace's embarrassment. "It's not you. People tell me things. Do you know that's why I do what I do? When I was a teenager, my best friend confessed she'd been sexually abused by her step-dad. She never told anyone else because she didn't think they'd believe her. I felt helpless and didn't like it. It brought back a million terrible memories from my childhood."

"Oh no," Jace said, not ready for someone else to confess they'd been sexually abused. Dealing with Jimmy had been enough for one lifetime.

"It's nothing like that," Tyler said, reassuring Jace as if he realized how his words sounded. "When I was little, I had an extremely abusive mom. I don't remember much about it because I had an awesome dad who kept me away from her. Unfortunately, my younger brother wasn't so lucky. My friend's confession reminded me of how helpless I'd felt when I couldn't help him. We had different dads, you see. He was the unlucky one." Tyler snorted. "Now it's almost funny I ever thought becoming a cop and joining the Exploited and Endangered Children's Division would change anything."

"Why is it funny?" Jace asked, engrossed in the conversation.

An acerbic-looking smile touched Tyler's lips. "Every day I wake up feeling more helpless and useless than the day before. There're way more kids out there than I can help."

Jace's eyes stung at the honesty in Tyler's voice. "That's sad."

Tyler shrugged again and his entire demeanor changed. "Wow. I ruined that moment, didn't I? Here, you gave me the perfect opening to tell you how much I'd love to be inside you. In fact, I don't think I've wanted anyone as much in years. Instead, I started talking about work. Obviously, I'm hopeless."

In spite of himself, Jace snorted. "In a way, I'm glad you changed the subject."

"Why's that?" Tyler asked as he brought his drink to his lips.

Jace was the one who shrugged this time. "Who knows what I might've said next? A thousand confessions raced to my tongue. If I'd kept on, I might've ended up too embarrassed to look at you again."

Tyler's mouth lifted in one corner, becoming the sexiest smirk Jace had ever seen. "You shouldn't be embarrassed with me. Not ever. I should confess, I'm pretty fucking kinky. After one night with me, you might not ever blush over anything else again."

There was something wrong with Jace's breathing. He sucked in a deep breath, trying to calm his racing heart. Nothing worked. Tyler's expression shifted again, going from wicked to cynical. He nodded toward a nearby table. "Now that guy should be embarrassed. He's been watching the game on his phone the whole night while his wife picks at her food. Nothing's worse than being lonely when you're not alone. I give it six months before she finds someone who appreciates her."

Jace glanced over. Sure enough, there was a guy wearing a football jersey sitting with a woman dressed for a night on the town. He was staring at his phone. She looked miserable. Jace hadn't noticed anyonc clsc around thcm sincc the moment they'd sat down. If anyone had asked, he would've sworn Tyler hadn't either. The man hadn't looked away from Jace all night.

"It's part of my job," Tyler explained, as if reading Jace's mind. "I always notice everything around me and take in the smallest details."

Jace was fascinated. "What else have I missed while you held my attention?"

A line appeared between Tyler's eyes. "I didn't mean to make you feel as if you haven't had my full and undivided attention."

Before he could stop it from happening, Jace rolled his eyes. "I don't feel that way at all." Jace winked. "Aren't you supposed to be good at reading people?"

Tyler sat forward. The way he focused on Jace made Jace feel like the rest of the world slipped away. "I'm very good at a lot of things."

Jace's blood sang. This man would make Jace beg. He felt it in his bones. "Then what else have I missed?" Jace asked again.

Tyler's smile said he was about to blow Jace's mind.

Jace had never been more intrigued by

anyone.

Tyler's gaze flickered toward a server across the room. "That waiter is stealing tips from the rest of the staff and 'forgot' to return a credit card to a customer earlier."

Jace bit his lip to keep from smiling. "Go on."

Challenge lit Tyler's eyes. "There're two women sitting behind me."

With a quick glance, Jace confirmed Tyler's claim. "And?"

"They've been friends for years. One just broke things off with her boyfriend because there was no spark. The other one is barely stopping herself from doing permanent damage to her vision from all the eye rolls she's holding back."

The more detailed Tyler's story

became, the more suspicious Jace grew. "How could you possibly know that?"

Tyler smiled. Jace wanted to lick him. "Because she said as much when she called her husband while the other girl was in the restroom."

"Hmmm," Jace hummed, barely hiding his skepticism. "Anything else?"

"You haven't gone out with anyone else since kicking Jimmy to the curb. My guess is the two of you never slept together. Even though you know he's a fucked-up mess, you still think the fault lies with you somehow. I haven't figured out why yet."

Tyler's claim was like getting punched in the chest. Jace sat back in his chair— winded. "Maybe we should go."

If Tyler was the least bit put off by Jace's wounded tone, he didn't show it. In fact, the man's gaze turned hotter. "We should definitely go. You need someone to show you how desirable you are. I can't do that here."

Jace wasn't so sure that was true. The man did a damn good job of making Jace feel wanted with only his stare. Tyler watched Jace like he'd be the man's next meal.

"Okay." Holy fuck. Had he just said that? Thankfully, they were still sitting inside the restaurant. Jace had plenty of time to change his mind. There were a thousand reasons he should stop this now. Tyler may as well be Jimmy's father. Even though Jace had met Tyler several months before tonight, Tyler was—for the most part—a stranger. Not to mention, Jace wasn't looking for another man to make him feel worthless. He was done trying to please someone else.

Jace glanced over at the married

couple beside them. He didn't want to end up like them. A bitter smile twisted his lips, matching his heart. At some point, he'd turned hard and unfeeling. That was probably the real reason Jimmy hadn't wanted him. From what Jace heard, Jimmy's new man, Eli, was sweet and innocent. He probably gave Jimmy all the warm and fuzzies. Fuckers. An inner sigh ran through Jace's head. In all truth, he hoped they were happy. After all, someone should be.

"Are you ignoring me now?"

At Tyler's question, Jace tore his gaze away from the couple beside them. "No," he said, not bothering to speak quietly. "I was wondering where that lady got her gorgeous shoes and sort of wishing she'd get up and walk out. Maybe then her date would give her the attention she deserves."

The woman snorted. Jace met her gaze

and winked. A glance passed between them. An understanding. Life sucked ass and not in a good way.

Chuckling, Tyler stood. "I'd better get you out of here before you start trouble. When I pictured you in handcuffs tonight, it wasn't because you were getting arrested."

Longing hit with a vengeance. Jace stumbled to his feet. If there was any chance Tyler wasn't joking, Jace wanted it. He was already half hard at the thought.

*

Tyler cursed himself for the idiot he was all the way back to Jace's house. Jace wasn't a wilting flower, but he was bitter as hell. Disappointment in life bled from his every pore.

"I had a great time tonight," Tyler said

as he opened Jace's car door. "Am I still invited inside or did you come to your senses yet?"

Jace's sexy eyes flashed with mischief. "Kiss me and then I'll decide if I'm impressed enough to keep you around a little longer."

Tyler bit the inside of his cheek to keep from laughing. "Your bravado is beautiful."

"Kiss me before I lose it," Jace whispered, sounding breathless.

The space between them disappeared before Tyler realized he'd moved. Their bodies collided. Tyler's caught fire. Jace fit perfectly against him. The way Jace watched him as if he held his breath—anticipating—had Tyler's lust skyrocketing. Despite the man's jaded outlook on life, there was something innocent about Jace. Tyler wanted to taste it on his tongue. He thought to move slow, giving Jace time to back out. Tyler didn't want Jace turning him down.

His fingers splayed across Jace's cheek. For a split second, he was captivated by their differences. Jace's skin was a few shades lighter than his dark hue. Tyler's hands appeared rougher than usual against Jace's unblemished body. He dipped his head. Jace met him halfway. Their lips touched. Tyler was lost to Jace's kiss.

The man was a nibbler. Deepening their kiss never lasted long. Jace kept backing away and drawing Tyler's bottom lip between his teeth, as if he couldn't get enough. There was no slow burn. Tyler was ready to fuck Jace standing up, against the truck, and in the middle of Jace's driveway.

A sound, somewhere between a moan and a growl, came from the back of Jace's throat. Tyler's knees weakened. An image of Jace on his knees, making that noise around Tyler's dick, flared to life in Tyler's mind. Jace wasn't one-night stand material. He was the kind of guy a man settled down with. The type he wanted to come home to every night. Tyler had no business touching him, tainting him. There was a huge list of reasons he should stop. He didn't.

"I want to peel these clothes from you and fuck you right here."

Jace swayed on his feet. "Oh, God."

"Let's go inside, Jace. Keep me for a few more hours. I can make you scream."

Jace's eyes fluttered open. The gorgeous irises that captured his attention from the start held him captive once more.

Instead of answering, Jace linked his fingers through Tyler's and tugged, leading him inside. The man was a fool. Tyler would eat him alive. Since Jace was obviously willing to let that happen, he wasn't turning Jace down. Tyler drew a steady breath as Jace unlocked the door. His muscles tensed. Patience was a thing of the past.

Jace glanced over his shoulder as they cleared the doorway. "Can I get you something—"

In one quick motion, Tyler kicked the door closed behind him and took Jace to the floor, cutting off whatever Jace had been about to say. He hadn't been lying earlier. Tyler loved sex. The kinkier the better. Jace's lips had been tempting him all night. He wanted to fuck them. To his surprise—somehow—Tyler was the one who ended up on his back while Jace tore at his clothes. After Tyler's shirt disappeared, Jace sat back on his heels while straddling Tyler's hips and pulled his shirt off. God. Damn. Tyler nearly swallowed his tongue. The man's body was perfect—cut in all the right places. Too late, he remembered where Jimmy had met Jace. They fought the same MMA circuit. He'd thought his dick couldn't get any harder. Tyler had been wrong. It leaked at the sight of Jace above him, taking what he wanted.

Jace loosened Tyler's belt. He glanced down as if surprised by its weight. Fuck. Tyler hadn't thought about his gun and handcuffs. He was a detective all the time. It was second nature. For other people, it could be off-putting. Jace stood. Tyler's heart dropped. He wished he hadn't been so engrossed in Jace he'd forgotten he was armed. There were lots of people who didn't like to be near a gun. Except Jace didn't back away. He held his hand out to help Tyler stand.

"Come on, darling. I don't do carpet burn for anyone. Not even someone as sexy as you."

Relief washed over him as he accepted Jace's hand and stood. He wasn't getting turned away, only relocated. Tyler held tight to Jace's fingers as the man led him through the house. It wasn't a huge place, but it was nice. Tyler didn't possess the mental capacity to absorb his surroundings right now. All he could concentrate on was the way the muscles moved in Jace's back when he walked. It should be illegal for anyone to be so sexy. Tyler bet everyone tripped over themselves to get this man's attention. Right now, Tyler was who Jace had chosen to bring home. He wouldn't let the man down.

Jace's bed came into view. It was high—like high enough he'd damn near need a step to get up in the thing, but perfect for bending Jace over. Reaching behind him, Tyler unsnapped his handcuffs before pulling them from his belt. Without giving Jace time to realize his plan, Tyler clapped them around the man's wrist.

"Now's your chance to back down," Tyler said before reaching for the man's free arm.

A hum came from the back of Jace's throat, making Tyler's dick leak. "I'm not that easy to scare."

"We'll see," Tyler said, clicking the other bracelet around Jace's wrist, trapping the man's arms behind his back. He should've tried to be at least a little romantic, considering it was their first time. Tyler didn't hold back. He nearly ripped the zipper out of Jace's jeans as he peeled them down the man's legs. Before he knew how it happened, Tyler had Jace bent over the edge of the bed, ass cheeks spread and tonguing the man's asshole. It was Jace's fault. He didn't hide his pleasure. The sounds he made and the way he rocked against Tyler's face was addictive.

Saliva ran down Tyler's hands as he fucked Jace with his fingers. Tyler wasn't the least bit gentle. His teeth sank into Jace's ass cheek hard enough to draw blood. He couldn't stop. His dick was climbing out his open pants. Jace's pre-cum combined with Tyler's spit. It was rough, raw, and dirty. Tyler experienced a real moment of fear that he might not ever want to leave. He had one fucking condom with him and already knew that wouldn't be enough. Jace was the type of man he could fuck all night.

Tyler shed his pants and found the condom in his wallet. It was lubricated, but he'd also made sure Jace was well soaked. With one hand holding the man's cuffs, Tyler used the other to guide his way inside Jace.

"Goddamn, Jace. Fuck." He couldn't be quiet. "You feel so good." Tyler's eyes fell closed as Jace's tight heat pulled him farther in. "Seriously, you've already got me ready to explode. I knew you'd be amazing. Anyone who made you feel unwanted is insane," Tyler said, between licking and sucking the side of Jace's neck. "I can't remember the last time I was this hard."

"Tyler."

It was one word, barely whispered. Yet it sent Tyler into a frenzy. He tugged at

Jace's cock, determined to make the man fly while pounding Jace's tight ass. Jace's muscles tensed, proving how close he was to the edge, and nearly taking Tyler's knees out as he tightened around Tyler's cock. When Jace finally exploded, his ass convulsed, milking Tyler's dick. He held still, hoping the man didn't cripple him for life even as Jace's orgasm triggered his own. Wave after wave of ecstasy pulled loud gasps from Tyler. His lips brushed Jace's sweat-soaked skin and words slipped from Tyler he couldn't control. He praised the man wrecking his body and swore he'd make him come again before the night ended. It wasn't empty talk. Before Tyler finally set Jace free from the cuffs and they fell into an exhausted heap of legs and arms into Jace's bed, Tyler had done his damnedest to ruin Jace for all others. God knew, Jace had already ruined him.

*

Cool air brushing his bare ass pulled Jace from the sleep of the dead. A smile tugged at the corners of his mouth before his eyes opened. It was darker than he expected. His gaze moved to the clock. Only an hour had passed since he'd cried "uncle." Light peeked around the closed bathroom door, casting just enough glow on the room for Jace to see Tyler gathering his clothes to leave. It was obvious by his slow movements that he was trying not to wake Jace. The muscles in Jace's stomach twisted. Tyler was seriously sneaking out on him. Part of Jace wanted to throw the covers back and demand Tyler leave like a real man if he wanted to go. The rest of Jace was resigned. As much as Jace had wanted Tyler to be different, turned out he wasn't. In truth, Tyler wasn't to blame. The problem was Jace. There was something fundamentally wrong with him—something that kept men from caring about him. As much as he tried to work on himself, convincing himself he was worth more than the people he surrounded himself with, men kept proving him wrong. It never hurt less—learning every horrible thing ever said to him, putting him down, was merely putting him in his place—undeserving of love.

Chapter 2

Three weeks later...

Jace didn't need to look at a calendar to know exactly how many days had passed since the last time he'd seen the man crossing the room. This was the last place he expected to see Tyler. The giant man leading him through Smith Brothers Fight Club stood a foot taller than everyone else, just as Tyler did. That made them easy to spot. Any other time, Jace may've made a run for it. Since Jimmy's engagement had just been announced to the club, and Jimmy stared at him with the only hint of apology Jace would ever get, Jace's brain wasn't working at full capacity. It had been less than a year since they'd split. Jace's current shock had nothing to do with that detail. It was the sure knowledge Jace would spend the rest of his life alone that glued Jace's feet to the ground, and then, Tyler had appeared, as if to emphasize how pathetic Jace was.

As Jace looked on, Tyler joined the celebration surrounding Jimmy and Eli. Jace couldn't tear his gaze from the smile stretching Tyler's lips. The man was happy—like Jace meant nothing. As if he felt Jace's stare, Tyler glanced over Jimmy's shoulder. Their gazes met. Tyler's smile slipped from his face like melting butter. For a moment, Tyler continued to hold Jace's stare even as his mouth kept moving, holding up his end of the conversation with Jimmy. Then the moment passed, and Tyler looked away, dismissing him. Funny, that small gesture hurt more than watching Tyler sneak away in the middle of the night. Jace grabbed his things. He couldn't do this. While skirting the edge of the gym, he tried making a break for it, hoping to slip away unnoticed. Two people stopped him, trying to lure him into a chat before he made his getaway. He knew everyone's hearts were in the right place. They all thought he was running away because his ex had just announced his impending marriage to someone else, but Jace wanted to get the fuck out of there before Tyler looked at him again. The man didn't need to speak to him to fuck with Jace's head. Jace did that all on his own.

His car came into view. "Jace, hold up." Jace's eyes fell closed at the sound of Tyler's voice. He was in hell. There was no other explanation for the nightmare this day had become. Jace picked up his pace, hoping Tyler would take a hint and leave him be. It didn't happen. "Seriously, Jace. Hold on a minute. I need to talk to you."

The day's events crashed down on

Jace's shoulders, bringing with it a swell of pure rage. Without thought, Jace turned on Tyler. "What do you want, Tyler?"

His open hostility had Tyler taking a step back as if shocked by Jace's tone. The man was a goddamn idiot. He'd fucked Jace and then ran for the hills but still expected a jovial greeting. Well, fuck him. Jace barely stopped himself from saying as much.

"It's not what you think."

"Really?" Jace said, infusing as much sarcasm as he could into the question. "What do I think?"

"That I got what I wanted and disappeared. Now I'm here taunting you with my presence—like you didn't matter. But, I swear, it's really not like that. I like you a lot, Jace. Way more than I should."

Jace stopped himself from crossing his arms over his chest, protecting his heart by force of will alone. Damned if Tyler hadn't named off every single fucking thing Jace was thinking. Hell would freeze before Jace admitted it. "I'm still waiting for you to tell me how it isn't like that."

Tyler looked panicked—like he hadn't expected Jace to press. He gave Jace a short nod as if he'd come to a decision. Jace hoped he'd chosen to be honest, because he'd been fed enough lies over the years. He didn't need a new man to shove shit down his throat. "All right, I guess—in a way—it is like that."

Okay. That hurt.

"But you do matter," Tyler added. "It's just that... Jimmy matters more."

Jesus. Really? Jace could've gone his whole life without this discussion.

"I'm not expressing myself well. See, like just now, Jimmy called me family, and I don't want to fuck that up, but I do like you, and fuck."

Enraged didn't begin to explain how Jace felt. His eye twitched. As he tried calling his temper under control, Jace ran his tongue over his teeth. Going to jail wasn't on his to-do list for the day. Tyler was cop; even off duty, Jace would probably get twice the time if he killed him right here. He knew the right thing would be to walk away. Jace had never been accused of showing good sense when it came to his heart.

"Here's the thing," Jace said, surprising even himself with how steady his voice sounded. "You knew I used to date Jimmy before you fucked me. It's not like you found out who I was after the fact. So... I'm not the fucking idiot you obviously take me for." Jace was beyond caring they were airing their business to all the people on the street. He needed to have his say. God knew, he never intended to see this bastard again after today. "You made a conscious decision to fuck me and walk away. This isn't you trying to do right by someone you care about. You planned all along to have both—me for one night without ruining what little relationship you have with Jimmy."

Tyler's expression gave nothing away. It didn't matter. Jace didn't need Tyler's thoughts. It was his own feelings Jace would have to live with when he walked away from Tyler. He already knew he would look back on this moment in shame if he didn't speak his mind now. "What you didn't consider is this," Jace added. "Not only does Jimmy not give two shits about me, or you, for that matter, but after you snuck out on me, you never had a shot at a second night with me. Following me out here gained you nothing." Because he was done and didn't care to hear anything else Tyler had to say, Jace turned away.

"Hold up, Jace. I'm sorry."

Jace didn't bother slowing. "Fuck you, Tyler," he called over his shoulder. "Oh, and by the way, Jimmy has been standing six feet behind you this entire time." Jace almost hated he missed Tyler's reaction to the news, but he couldn't look at Tyler a second longer. He thought he knew what it was like to be pissed off at someone. Tyler had shown him a whole new level of rage.

*

At Jace's words, Tyler's eyes fell closed. He tilted his chin to the sky even as his shoulders fell. There wasn't a doubt in

Tyler's mind Jace had known the entire time Jimmy was there and intentionally ensured Jimmy heard every word. Jace was a little evil. Goddamn. Tyler loved that. If Jimmy's stare wasn't burning a hole in the back of Tyler's head, he'd be hard as steel right now.

"Well, that was a dick move."

Jimmy sounded calm. There was that. Since Jimmy was the most hot-tempered person Tyler knew, that was saying a lot. There was nothing else for it; Tyler turned and met Jimmy's stare. He had one arm slung over Eli's shoulders, holding the man tight against his side. Eli looked as if he too braced himself for Jimmy's explosion.

"Which part?" Tyler asked, because he'd be damned if he'd incriminate himself.

"All of it," Jimmy said, still sounding eerily unaffected by the entire scene. "But, mostly, I was referring to what you did to Jace. I mean, I'm a fucked-up mess. At least I have an excuse for not being what the guy needed when we were together. That said, I never fucked him, so... you, you're just a dick." He shook his head. "Of all people, you should know sex is a weapon. When used just right, it can destroy a person. Congratulations on demolishing a genuinely nice guy."

Tyler felt sick. He didn't think there'd ever been a day when he'd lost so many people's respect all at one time. Of all the days for Jimmy to be the levelheaded one. "You should be screaming at me right now."

Jimmy's lips twisted, as if Tyler left a bad taste in his mouth. "Eli doesn't like it when I yell. Besides, today has been one of

49

the best days of my life. Not even you can ruin it. You should go after Jace."

Eli nodded, reminding Tyler of his presence. "You should. He didn't deserve that."

He hadn't, but Tyler was in a tough spot. He liked Jace. A lot. Way more than anyone he'd met in years. Jace was Jimmy's ex. Jimmy was all the family Tyler had. Fuck.

As if reading his mind, Jimmy nodded toward Tyler's truck. "Go on. The longer you let this fester, the worse it'll be. You have my blessing or what the fuck ever you're waiting on."

Tyler chewed his bottom lip, trying to decide what to do. They had more they needed to talk about other than Jace. In the past few weeks, Tyler had made some real progress with Jimmy. Hell, not ten minutes earlier, Jimmy had called him family. As much as he craved Jace, he didn't want to lose this connection with Jimmy for someone who probably wouldn't want him six months from now. After all, he worked late hours, was surly as hell, and would make Jace tired. Goddamn. He'd also fuck Jace until the man couldn't stand, proudly hold his hand wherever they went, and do some naughty shit to those sexy lips. Jimmy was right. He needed to go after him.

"So we're cool?" Tyler asked, still unsure of Jimmy's odd calm.

Jimmy features hardened. "No. We're so not cool. In fact, we may never be cool again, but that has nothing to do with Jace or the fact we used to date. I couldn't care less who the man fucks. This is about you screwing with someone's head. I thought you were better than that."

51

Without giving Tyler time to formulate a response, Jimmy steered Eli away. Eli flashed Tyler a sad smile as they passed. Damn, he really liked that kid. Eli was the only reason Jimmy had given him a shot recently. Tyler wanted to growl. He'd known messing with Jace was a bad idea. He just hadn't been able to stop himself. Jimmy didn't care about a lot of shit—most shit, actually. But any hint of manipulation of anyone he cared about was a deal-breaker for him. Goddamn it. Tyler honestly hadn't meant to hurt Jace. He'd come here today, touring the club in hopes of getting closer to the man. Tyler was in a fucked-up position. For a full five minutes, Tyler stood on the sidewalk while staring at nothing. He had no idea where to go from here. All he knew was that he really wanted to talk to Jace again, even if Jace yelled at him while it happened.

* * *

"New patient waiting."

Jace flashed his assistant, Paige, a smile. "I'll be right there." He grabbed one more stack of gauze before leaving the stockroom with his haul balanced in his arms. He kept his gaze locked on the tiny piles of supplies as he stepped back inside his exam room. He was always torn between making several trips and risking everything falling onto the floor. A smile exploded across his face as he dumped the supplies safely on the counter. It was the little triumphs in life.

"Hey, babe."

Jace's knees weakened even as his spine stiffened. It was insane how he knew Tyler's voice after only one night together. Yet Jace felt certain he could find the man in the dark and in a crowd of hundreds by his voice alone. Jace drew a deep breath for courage and turned. Even sitting in a dentist chair with blue paper clipped around his neck, Tyler looked fucking delicious. It wasn't fair.

"Tyler. What brings you in today?"

Tyler toyed with the paper resting on his chest. If Jace wasn't mistaken, the man fought back a blush. "Oh, you know, getting my teeth cleaned."

For some reason Jace couldn't explain, the heavy humor in Tyler's voice pissed him off—like Tyler thought Jace was a joke. "Fine," Jace said, moving his tray closer and taking a seat at Tyler's head. "How long has it been since your last cleaning?"

The humor melted from Tyler's expression. He cleared his throat. "Um. I'm a little behind. My insurance changed and no longer covers my old dentist. So, maybe eight months?"

Jace nodded, keeping his professional face in place. Paige stepped into the room. Her presence helped Jace keep his shit together. "Do you have his x-rays?" he asked Paige while trying to pretend Tyler was just another patient.

"Yes, sir. I'm pulling them up now."

Jace kept his gaze plastered to the computer screen behind Tyler's head, refusing to look Tyler's way. Images appeared across the screen. Jace slipped into work mode.

"Everything looks good," he said as he switched on the light over the chair and adjusted it. Jace pulled up his mask and focused on Tyler. "Turn your head this way," Jace said unnecessarily since Tyler was already focused on him.

"Goddamn, Jace. Your eyes are even sexier in this light. I didn't think that was possible."

Jace ignored Tyler's remark, but he could feel Paige's stare boring into the top of his head. "Open up."

As soon as Tyler did as told, Jace retreated into the familiar. "Suction, please?" Jace said, knowing Paige would be right where he needed her. They'd worked together for nine years now. She was his best friend, and—unfortunately— she knew all about what happened with the bastard sitting in Jace's chair.

He finished one side. "Turn your head toward Paige. I'm starting on the other side."

"You're being amazingly gentle, considering how much you hate me," Tyler said before Jace had a chance to get his instruments back in his mouth.

Jace went back to work, stopping Tyler from saying anything more. "That's because I'm a professional," Jace said, letting some bitterness slip into his tone. Paige glanced between them, looking worried. She knew Jace well enough to know he'd never be hostile toward just anyone. Jace tried to stop his rage from building. It didn't happen. "Why should I let some guy who used me for sex interfere with my job? After all, you're not special. Everyone treats me that way." Jace never looked away from his task during his tirade. "Of course, my mom always told me—act like a whore, and people will treat you as one." He set his tools aside, slamming them down harder than intended before snapping off his gloves. "We're done here. Paige will brush some fluoride on your teeth. You can eat and drink right away, but don't brush for twelve hours." He stood and headed for the door. "Dr. Swanson will want to check out your teeth before you leave. Make sure you set up your next appointment at the front desk."

"Jace."

Jace didn't slow. Why wouldn't this man leave him alone? He didn't want Jace. Tyler had made that abundantly clear. There was no reason whatsoever for Tyler to keep up this torture.

"Jace," Tyler repeated.

Paige snapped, "Sir, he's already told you he's a professional. I'm not. I will stick this straight into your gums if you move again."

An evil smile pulled at Jace's lips as he moved away. Damn, he loved that woman. Maybe they should move in together and adopt fifteen cats? Jace's smile turned bitter once more. He was allergic to cats. Seemed he would be growing old alone after all.

*

Showing up at Jace's work was strike two as far as Tyler was concerned. The gym had been bad enough, but the dental visit had been brutal and not well thought out. Jace had kept him quiet by being in his mouth the whole time, and not in a good way. Once he'd left the room, his she-devil protector had taken over Tyler's torment. She'd readjusted the light, ensuring it shined in Tyler's eyes before stabbing him several times in the gums with some kind of wooden swab. If her fury hadn't been directed at him, Tyler might've found it funny.

Now he was on to plan "C." That was why he was knocking on the man's door at seven in the morning on a Saturday. He knew Jace didn't work weekends. Tyler was off for the first time in forever. Come hell or high water, Jace would spend time with him today. A guy who couldn't be older than twenty finally opened the door. Tyler's mind went blank. It hadn't occurred to him Jace might be with someone else.

The guy's eyebrows rose when Tyler didn't say anything. "I'm assuming you're here to see Jace."

Tyler couldn't look away from the guy's nose ring. Under no circumstances could Tyler picture Jace with a guy who wore a ring in his nose. "Uh, yeah," Tyler finally stuttered. "Is he around?"

Nose Ring Guy waved him inside. "I'm Adam," he said as he closed the door behind Tyler.

"Tyler," Tyler said while still trying to decide who this guy was to Jace.

Adam immediately reopened the door. "Get out. Uncle Jace will kill me if he sees I've let you in."

Tyler didn't budge. Instead, he snapped his fingers as he realized who Adam was. "You're the makeup artist. Did you get the internship?"

Adam's entire demeanor changed. "I did. Thank you for asking. Jace is getting sick of hearing me talk about it. I leave for New York in three days. I still can't believe it." Adam was near to dancing in place in his excitement.

"Are you going alone?"

Adam nodded and pressed a hand to his stomach. "I'm nervous as heck. It's a huge city and I've never been on my own, but I'm too thrilled to care."

Tyler bit back the desire to lecture Adam on ways to keep himself safe. Instead, he changed the subject. "Do you live here?"

"Yes, he does," Jace said, pulling Tyler's attention toward the kitchen doorway. He had no idea how long Jace had been standing there, but the man didn't look happy to see Tyler.

Adam closed the door. He flashed Tyler an apologetic smile. "Sorry, Uncle Jace. I didn't realize who it was until I'd already invited him inside."

Everything else fell away as Tyler stared at Jace. Dressed in gray sweatpants and a black T-shirt, he looked lickable. Jace never looked bad or out of place, but this relaxed version of Jace was hot as hell.

Jace's gaze never wavered from Tyler,

even as he directed his words at Adam. "It's not your fault. Tyler has a way of sneaking into places where he's not wanted."

Ouch.

"I think I'll go," Adam said, making his escape down the hall and proving his intelligence.

Tyler waited until they were alone before speaking. "You have a way of dodging my attempts to apologize."

Jace's expression gave no hint to his thoughts. "Are you apologizing?"

"I'm trying," Tyler said, refusing to let Jace's less than welcoming tone deter him. "I'm sorry, Jace. Truly. I was wrong. You should punch me in the nuts. Please don't, but you should."

For a moment, Jace eyed him, as if

assessing his earnestness. "That's it? You're not offering excuses?"

"I have none," Tyler admitted.

Jace nodded. "Fine. You're forgiven."

"That's it?" Tyler asked, stealing Jace's earlier question. "No cutting remarks or getting even?"

Jace shook his head. "I'm not a vindictive person."

"Does that mean I can take you to breakfast?"

"No."

Tyler blinked at the finality in Jace's tone. "Oh." He swiped his palms on his jeans. Jace might not be a vindictive person, but he was obviously still done with Tyler.

Jace released a loud sigh. "I was in the middle of breakfast when you showed up.

It's not much. Fruit and muffins, but there's enough for another person if you'd like to join me."

Tyler headed for the kitchen, accepting whatever time in Jace's company the man was willing to mete out. His steps slowed as he crossed the threshold of the kitchen. It was an open style and huge. The countertops appeared to be marble and all the appliances were something Tyler expected to see inside an upscale restaurant. There were several types of fruit, an open container of yogurt, and muffins spread out on an oak table.

Jace grabbed another plate, spoon, and fork before motioning for Tyler to sit. "You can sit wherever."

Since there was only one plate on the table, Tyler chose the chair next to it. Jace set the plate he was carrying in front of Tyler before snagging his own plate and moving to the opposite side of the table. Tyler swallowed down his laughter. Point taken.

"What are your plans for the day?" Tyler asked, hoping to get a firm read on where he stood with Jace.

Jace shrugged as he tore off a piece of muffin. "I just got home from the gym, so I guess I'll take a shower before helping Adam pack. We don't have much time left to get him ready to go."

"Would you like some help?" Tyler paused for half a heartbeat before adding, "With the packing, not the shower." It took all his willpower not to tack on his willingness to help there as well. Tyler imagined Jace wouldn't appreciate the offer.

Jace's face scrunched up in confusion. Tyler had to take a deep breath to control his body's reaction to the sight. Damn. Everything about Jace was sexy. "Why would you want to help? Packing sucks."

"Because I like spending time with you and I'll take whatever I can get."

After swiping the crumbs from his hands, Jace sat back in his chair and eyed Tyler with open suspicion.

Adam dumped some dishes in the sink, pulling their attention his way. "You should let him help. He's only trying to be nice, Jace." Adam walked away as if he hadn't gotten involved.

Tyler's gaze landed on Jace once more. He kept his features carefully blank, not wanting Jace to sense an ounce of gloating.

Jace pushed away from the table. "It's his stuff. If Adam wants you to help, then whatever. Finish your breakfast," Jace ordered. "I'll grab a shower and we can get started."

Tyler dutifully chewed his muffin, determined Jace wouldn't see his triumph. After all, Jace was headed to the shower alone. That meant Tyler hadn't won shit yet.

* * *

Between the three of them, it took no time at all to get Adam squared away. Tyler genuinely liked the boy. He was witty and upbeat. He'd do well on his own. Still, he was way too pretty to be walking the streets of New York by himself, but that was the side of Tyler that had seen too much, talking. Tyler kept his concerns to himself.

"Did you talk to Jimmy and work things out?"

Tyler shook his head. "He's not answering my calls or texts. Eli is still talking to me, but I'm not sure Eli has ever been mean to anyone in his life."

Jace stood and grabbed his keys. "Come on."

Even though he had no clue what was happening, Tyler stood. "Okay. Where are we going?"

"To fix things with Jimmy," Jace answered, as if it was as simple as saying it.

Tyler dutifully followed Jace into the garage. When Jace reached the driver's side door of his car, the black BMW M4 automatically unlocked. Tyler opened the door for Jace. He watched the man slide behind the wheel while beating down his hunger. Jesus. It was like he was always on when Jace was around. Before he could do something stupid—like talk—Tyler closed the door and moved to join Jace inside. The car was nice—like way more than Tyler expected nice. He clasped his hands in his lap to keep from running them over the soft leather.

Unfortunately, keeping his fingers locked together didn't stop his lips from moving. "I get the impression you make a lot more money than I do."

Jace's chuckle let Tyler know he wasn't bothered. "It's a good thing too. Raising a teenager on my own wasn't cheap."

"You raised Adam?" Tyler had no idea why he asked, since Jace had just said as much. He was more surprised than anything. He'd never had so much in common with anyone. Tyler wanted to know everything.

Jace nodded as he backed out of the garage. "My sister and her husband were killed in a car accident eight years ago.

Adam was with them at the time but didn't even have a scratch. Since my parents were already well past retirement age when Adam was born, and Evie hated Brock's parents, I agreed to be Adam's godfather." Jace shook his head. "No one ever thinks that title will get called in. Mine did."

Tyler shook his head—amazed by this gorgeous man. "How old was Adam?"

"Twelve. He didn't say a word for three years afterward. Trauma from what he'd witnessed," Jace explained while keeping his gaze locked on the road. "But he's always been a great kid." He flashed Tyler a smile. "Even if I hadn't already been his godfather, I would've fought for him."

"That's because you're amazing."

Jace shook his head. "No. It's because he is."

All Tyler could do was shake his head. For the life of him, he couldn't understand why Jace didn't see what he'd just said was exactly what made him so fucking fantastic.

*

Jimmy's bar didn't open for another two hours. Jace expected he'd have to bang on the man's alleyway side door to get his attention. As they pulled in the parking lot, Jace realized that would be unnecessary. The front door stood open and loud music spilled out. Almost every parking space was already taken, forcing Jace to hunt for a place to park. Inside, boxes of liquor and kegs of beer sat stacked in every corner. Logan, the bar's manager, glanced up from the box he was unpacking as Jace and Tyler came through the door. The man possessed the lightest green eyes Jace had ever seen.

They always sparkled with laughter. Everyone liked Logan.

"Hey, Jace... and random stranger who I swear I've seen before. Are you looking for Jimmy or can I get you a drink? We're not officially open, but I'd make an exception for you," Logan said, adding a wink and making Jace blush. He knew it was a stupid reaction. Logan already had more men than he could handle and Jace wasn't interested anyhow, but there was no denying the man's charm.

"We're here for Jimmy. Is he around?"

Logan nodded toward the back. "He's in his office. You can head inside if you'd like."

Even though the place wasn't open yet for the day, it was packed to capacity with employees. Honestly, Jace hadn't realized so many people worked there. He weaved his way through people and boxes before circling the bar and heading for Jimmy's office. Tyler followed in his footsteps. Bottles clanked and the music was too loud to think straight, while employees laughed and talked over the noise.

Together, Jace and Tyler peeked inside Jimmy's office. It was empty. Jace backtracked until he found Logan. "Are you sure he's in there?"

Logan indicated walking with his fingers. "Walk around the desk," he yelled, sending Jace on his way again.

This time, Jace went inside the office. Before he'd completely circled the desk, he spotted two sets of legs sticking out from underneath. One set was propped on the office chair while the other legs were entangled in the first set. The closer he got, the bigger Jace's smile grew. Jimmy and Eli were on the floor, under the desk.

Eli's head was on Jimmy's chest. They shared a set of earbuds and were watching something on the laptop resting on Jimmy's stomach.

"I thought you didn't watch TV," Jace said by way of greeting.

Eli's smile was so damn sweet. Every time Jace saw him, Jace regretted every bitter feeling he'd had toward the man a little more. "We're listening to an audiobook while going over inventory lists," he explained to Jace.

"On the floor?" Tyler asked, announcing his presence.

Jimmy clicked a few buttons on the keyboard before pulling out his earbud. He motioned for Jace to take the laptop. After Jace relieved him of his burden, setting the computer on the desk, Eli climbed out. Jimmy followed.

"It's very loud in here today," Eli said, as if it explained everything.

The compassion written on Tyler's face let Jace know he understood what was going on, even if Jace didn't. "You should make Jimmy go out there and tell them to keep it down."

Eli shook his head, but Jimmy was the one who spoke up. "They're overworked and letting off steam." He tucked Eli under his arm. "Plus, it gives me an excuse to find a quiet spot with my baby."

A blush tinted Eli's cheeks at Jimmy's words, but he focused on Jace, as if determined not to leave Jace out. "We sold the bar in Nashville. Now we're in the process of moving all the inventory from that location to this location. It's overwhelming, but we're slowly winning the battle."

They were such a team. Every conversation was "us" and "we." Jace tried not to be jealous. They were a living example of his relationship goals. "That sounds like a lot of work, but the two of you can do anything." As Jace said the words, he realized he meant them. They were meant to be together.

"What brings you by?" Jimmy asked, sounding as if he was already at his limit of dealing with company for the day.

Jace gave him a short nod, letting him know he understood. "Tyler and I would like to apologize to you both for what happened outside the gym. It was your day. We were real assholes for causing drama." He could feel Tyler's stare boring into his skin, but Jace refused to look the man's way. Tyler would never get anywhere with Jimmy if he didn't start somewhere. Jace decided to the leave the man no choice in the matter. "We're thrilled you're getting married. You're perfect for each other, and we'd like to take you to lunch as a way of offering our congrats." It was dirty as hell using their engagement as a way of forcing Jimmy to spend time with Tyler. Jace wasn't above such things.

"Awwww, that's sweet," Eli said, trapping Jimmy further and making Jace wonder if it had been a purposeful move.

A muscle jumped in Jimmy's jaw.

Tyler was the first to break. "We didn't realize how busy you are. It doesn't have to be today."

The way Eli chewed his bottom lip, as if worried Jimmy might explode, had guilt gnawing at Jace's gut. Luckily, Jimmy caved before Jace broke.

"If Eli is okay with it, then whatever."

"Can we go somewhere quiet?"

Jace rushed to reassure him as relief flooded his veins. "Absolutely." Before now, he hadn't realized how gentle and somewhat vulnerable Eli was. The man made Jace feel like a bully, stampeding through everything to get his way.

After tossing around a few ideas, they settled on a small Italian restaurant where the lights were always kept low and the mood calm. With an agreement set to meet there in half an hour, Jace and Tyler climbed back into the car. That was as far as Jace made it before the need to know got the best of him.

"Okay, what the hell is up with Eli? I feel like I'm always one step away from making a complete ass of myself because there's some grand secret I'm not privy to."

Tyler's surprise couldn't have been

more evident at Jace's question. "I assumed, since you always talk to Eli as if he's your friend, you'd know all about him."

Jace shook his head. "I talk to everyone like I know them. It comes from years of working with the public. But, from your expression back there, I assumed you knew why he gives me an I-want-to-protect-him vibe."

Tyler buckled his seat belt as he answered, "I do, but not because anyone told me. Mostly, it's going on years of working with exploited and endangered kids." He met Jace's gaze. "Plus, I pulled all his info after I met him the first time." Tyler didn't sound ashamed.

"I have to know," Jace said, sounding every bit as gossipy as he felt.

A low chuckle rumbled from Tyler's

chest. It was hot and did something funny to Jace's stomach. "Horribly abused," Tyler said, killing all desire in Jace. "We're talking broken bones, concussions, starved, locked in rooms for days with not even a drop of water to drink. Every horrible thing you can think of one human doing to another, he suffered at the hands of people who should've loved him the most. His file says he had an older brother who committed suicide in front of him. Eventually, he ended up on the streets and fell off the radar until Jimmy."

"Oh my God." Jace couldn't even start the car. All he could do was stare at Tyler in horror. "Why didn't someone intervene? He should've been taken away from them and sent to live with a real family. His parents should be shot," Jace added, feeling more bloodthirsty by the minute.

For some reason Jace couldn't

understand, Tyler was smiling. "You're a good person," Tyler said, apropos to nothing as far as Jace was concerned. Tyler shook his head and sighed when Jace didn't respond to his praise. "A lot of kids fall through the cracks in the system. They never go to the doctor. When they do, it's never the same one twice. If teachers start asking questions, they're pulled from school and sent somewhere else or homeschooled. People who could and should intervene don't. Eli is the perfect example of someone failed by the system on every level."

Tyler fell silent. For an unguarded moment, Jace saw something dark in the man. Tyler looked away, staring at something in the distance when he spoke again. "There are lots of monsters in the world. Way more than there are good people. Almost everyone you meet, on a daily basis, is a piece of shit. You just don't realize it."

Damn, and here Jace thought he was the jaded one. "Does that include you?"

Tyler met his stare at the question. "Oh, babe. I'm the biggest of them all, because I hurt you."

Jace tore his gaze away and started the car. He was fine to talk about other people's issues, but his own—that shit cut too deep for such a beautiful day.

* * *

Somehow, Jace worked his magic and managed to keep Jimmy and Eli in their company the entire day. All Tyler had done was stare in amazement with each new idea. After lunch, he'd offered to introduce the pair to a friend of his who could officiate their wedding on short notice. Neither Jimmy nor Eli had a plan in place for the ceremony. All they knew was they wanted to be married before Jimmy's birthday next month.

Once that was done, Jace offered their services—free of charge—to help with the bar's inventory. Once there, Jace had monopolized Eli's time, leaving Jimmy no choice but to interact with Tyler. It had been nice. He'd never seen Jimmy as calm. Being with Eli was everything, it seemed, because Jimmy was a different man than the one Tyler raised. Tyler had never been more grateful for a few hours of someone's time.

When dinnertime came around, Eli offered to return the favor of lunch by taking them out to dinner. The suggestion left Tyler wondering if Jace had enlisted Eli's help with forcing Jimmy to spend time with Tyler. He wasn't sure why Jace had done so much, but—by the end of the night—Tyler couldn't stop staring at Jace in wonder. Tyler had never met anyone more amazing. As they arrived back at Jace's, Tyler found himself wishing he could stop time. He wasn't ready to leave Jace's company yet.

Even though Tyler's truck was parked at the curb, he followed Jace to the door. He wouldn't go inside, but he wanted to make sure Jace made it indoors safely. Plus, he needed to make the man understand how much he appreciated everything Jace had done. At the door, Jace turned and met his stare. Tyler had to say something quick before he begged Jace to keep him forever.

"Thank you for everything you did today."

Jace's nose crinkled. Tyler's stomach churned with hunger. "I didn't do anything."

"That's not true," Tyler argued. "You forced me on Jimmy, and you went with me, probably stopping him from killing me while it happened."

"Nah," Jace said, dismissing Tyler's praise. "You should thank Eli. Jimmy's never cared if I see him lose his shit. He's different with Eli—calmer." There was a sad note to Jace's voice—like he thought he'd failed Jimmy somehow.

Tyler had to fix it. "That's because you're strong."

A low laugh escaped Jace. "I appreciate you trying to make it better, but you don't have to. We were never serious, and he belongs with Eli."

"I'm being honest here," Tyler said, warming up to the topic. "See, like with me, Jimmy knows he can throw anything at all at me and I can take it. He's the same with you. He knows he won't knock you down. Eli, he's more like Jimmy. Jimmy can be real and raw with Eli, but at the same time, Eli brings out his protective side. They can let each other see all the places inside them they don't let anyone else see. Jimmy could never withstand being weak around me. It's no wonder he hates me."

Jace's focus never wavered. Tyler wanted to tell him everything. No one ever hung on his every word. Jace was now. "I don't think that's true."

A sad smile tugged at Tyler's lips. "Trust me. It's true, but it's not personal. Jimmy hates most everyone. The things he's been through..." Tyler paused, forced to swallow past the pain. "You can't imagine. Someone can't endure that much and walk away still seeing the best in people. No one can keep that much suffering inside and not lose their mind. I'm glad he found Eli. They make each other whole."

Jace nodded. "They're beautiful."

Tyler hated that Jace still sounded so damn sad. "That's not the only reason I'm glad they found each other."

"He's stopped drinking. That's a miracle."

"It is," Tyler agreed. "But that's not what I meant. If he hadn't met Eli, he may've found a way to win you back. That would've been a real loss for me."

Jace snorted. Even that was hot. "Yeah, you would've missed out on your one and only night of hot sex."

Tyler shook his head. "I would've missed out on a friend." Tyler took a step closer as he made the claim. He wanted to taste Jace's lips again with something akin to desperation. When Jace didn't jump away, Tyler moved even closer, praying Jace wouldn't back down.

Something dark passed over Jace's features. "Trust me, I'm no loss at all. It was good spending time with you today. I hope things work out between Jimmy and you."

In his shock, Tyler only watched as Jace disappeared inside. Jimmy had been so fucking right in his statement outside the gym. Sex was a weapon, and Tyler had done his part to demolish a good man.

Chapter 3

"Hey, Jace. There's a messenger here for you."

Jace glanced up from the paperwork he was entering in the computer and focused on Paige. "A messenger? Is that still a thing?"

Paige's light brown eyes danced with humor. "Apparently."

Curiosity brought Jace to his feet. "I thought they only existed in the movies. Just think about it," he said, heading for the front. "Email, texts, phone calls—why would anyone pay a messenger?"

Paige's tinkling laughter followed him down the hall. "Especially this one."

"What's that supposed to mean?" he asked over his shoulder.

"You'll see."

When Jace rounded the corner, his steps faltered. He tried holding back his laughter. The guy waiting for him was dressed like a chicken. No clue as to why, but there was no denying the bright feathers. The guy's face showed through the beak. He looked every bit as thrilled as a grown man should while dressed as a giant bird.

"You have a message for me?" Jace's question sounded strained as he fought back his laughter.

The man dug through his kangaroo-type pouch, because it seemed chickens from giant-birdland had those. He came out with a blue envelope. "If you don't like what's scratched inside, don't choke the messenger."

A snort escaped Jace before he could

call it back. He pursed his lips, hoping it wouldn't happen again. "Am I supposed to tip you? I'm sorry," he said, rushing to explain. "This is a first for me."

The dude's face was priceless. "Yeah, I'm wearing a chicken suit, so…"

"Point taken," Jace said, digging for his wallet. He felt everyone's eyes on him, even after the cranky bird left. With his head down and Paige's laughter following him down the hall, Jace escaped to his exam room to read his letter. Of course, there was no escaping Paige. Since he knew he wouldn't get out of telling her everything, he opened the note.

Jace,

I realized too late I still haven't asked for your number. A few months ago, at work, my partner got a message from this big chicken. We laughed our asses off for hours afterward. So I hoped this would brighten your day, or—at the very least—soften your she-protector against me.

Jace chuckled as he read Tyler's words. Paige had told him all about the way she'd tormented Tyler after Jace had left them alone.

Not only am I including my number in hopes you'll use it, I'm using this epic delivery method as my pass to say what I want. Here it goes—I've gotten nothing accomplished since our first date. All I do is stare into space and think about you. You check every box for me. Can I see you tonight? If I don't hear from you, I'll go away, but I'd love for you to give me a chance. — Tyler

Jace's cheeks ached. Even though he wasn't sure if he'd see Tyler again, he still dug his phone out and saved the man's number. Once he had it, Jace passed the

93

note Paige's way. He stared at Tyler's name on his phone while she read.

She snorted. "She-protector."

Jace's smile kicked up a notch.

"You know," Paige said, once finished. She handed the note back. "This guy is really chasing you. It's kind of sweet, in a ridiculous chicken suit kind of way. I'm not sure if I should tell you to make him squirm or snatch him up before he gets away."

"Yeah. I'm feeling the same way."

"Go with your gut," Paige said, giving his arm a push, as if it would help jar his mind. In a way, it did. Before even he accepted it was happening, Jace texted Tyler.

Jace: *What if I'd had a chicken phobia? I might've needed counseling.*

Tyler: *Ha! Number saved. I have you now.*

The problem was, Tyler had him from the moment he'd shown up on Jace's doorstep unannounced. It wasn't love. Jace didn't believe in insta-love. Thank God, since Tyler had sneaked out on him that first night. But they had a connection. They felt right, and that made Tyler dangerous. This man could and most likely would destroy him.

Tyler: *So? Tonight?*

Jace: *I'm helping Adam finish loading up his moving truck. He's leaving for New York in the morning. Maybe tomorrow night instead?*

Tyler: *So we're helping Adam load up his moving truck tonight?*

Paige's hot breath brushed Jace's neck as she read over his shoulder. He wanted to tell her to go away but knew it would be pointless.

"Tell him yes," she said, nearly blowing out his eardrum in her excitement.

Jace's fingers hovered over the buttons, hoping he wasn't making the biggest mistake of this life.

Jace: *It seems we are.*

Tyler: *See you at seven.*

It was done. All Jace could do now was pray he didn't end up a blubbering mess in a straitjacket.

*

Jace's body brushed against his as Jace tried to squeeze past him in the moving truck. It was the fifth time in the last hour. This helping Adam move shit was murder on Tyler's sanity. He'd never wanted anyone as much as he did Jace. This time of body-on-body connection, Tyler lost what little control he clung to. He took a step closer, pinning Jace. Jace's shocked expression transformed to one of pleasure when their gazes collided. Tyler's chest tightened at the sight of Jace's sweet brown eyes.

"You're so goddamn gorgeous. Why are you wasting your time with me?"

Jace's nervous-sounding chuckle brought a smile to Tyler's lips. "You're free labor."

If his intention had been to insult Tyler, Jace failed miserably. Tyler enjoyed their proximity too much. "I'll be your workhorse, babe. Use me," he begged.

The back door opened and Tyler stepped back, freeing Jace. Jace skittered away, obviously still unsure of Tyler.

"That's okay. I love watching that sexy ass run away," Tyler called at his back.

Adam's laughter filled the truck.

A smile that felt evil even to him stretched Tyler's lips. "Sorry not sorry," Tyler said, since he figured he should.

Adam shook his head. "I'm sure."

"Oh, hey," Tyler said, almost forgetting his need to talk to Adam. "This is for you," he said, holding out a small but powerful Taser. "Be careful. It delivers a punch, but I'd feel better if you had some type of protection while walking alone on the streets of New York."

Adam eyed the device. He clicked the safety off and pressed the button. Tyler was impressed when Adam didn't startle at the loud zapping sound it made. He clicked the safety back in place and met Tyler's stare.

"Thank you. I admit this makes me feel better. May I ask you a question?"

Tyler didn't hesitate. "Of course."

"Do you mean the things you say to Uncle Jace?"

If it had been anyone else, Tyler might've been offended. Adam's jade eyes held so much concern for the man who'd raised him, Tyler couldn't ignore his fears. "I never say things I don't mean."

Adam dipped his chin as if taking Tyler at his word. "That's good. He's been through a lot in the past few years, and he deserves someone nice."

"I'm not nice," Tyler said, rushing to correct Adam's assumptions. "I'm honest, but no—I'm not nice."

Adam winced. "That's too bad. The last thing Uncle Jace needs is someone else who hurts him."

Adam tried stepping around Tyler, heading back for the house. Tyler refused to let him pass. "Wait. What's that supposed to mean? I know Jimmy is— *was*—a heavy drinker, but he would never intentionally hurt anyone."

Adam's face screwed up, showing his

confusion. "I wasn't talking about Jimmy. I meant Jace's ex-husband."

"Ex-husband?" Even to Tyler's ears, he sounded dead.

Adam nodded. "I'm not surprised he didn't tell you. Brad did a real number on his head, always cheating with someone and telling Jace how he might stay faithful if Jace wasn't so fat. He loved telling him all about his extra-marital activities while stressing how no one else would ever want Jace because he was boring and ugly. It was sickening."

Tyler had a minute where his tongue wouldn't work. Rage had him expecting a full-blown stroke at any moment. Thankfully, Adam didn't seem to need him to hold up his end.

"Anyhow, about two years ago, Brad made a comment about how grown up and sexy I'd become. It was almost funny the instant transformation Jace underwent.

He walked back to their bedroom and gathered Brad's stuff. He started throwing all of it in the yard and calmly telling him to get the fuck out. It was pretty badass."

The back door opened and Adam's expression turned guilty. He slipped past Tyler and into the house before Tyler regained his wits.

Jace stacked another box on the pile. Tyler pounced, spinning the man in his arms and capturing Jace's mouth. To his surprise, Jace didn't fight him. Instead, a moan vibrated from the man's throat, caressing their entwined tongues.

"I'm sorry," Tyler said as he changed angles and came at the man again. His hands shaped the curve of Jace's ass before his grip tightened on the perfect globes. He hauled the man closer. His anger needed a balm. "You're seriously so goddamn sexy, I couldn't resist. Tell me to stop before I scar your nephew for life."

"He's a smart kid. He can cover his eyes," Jace said before giving back as good as he got. The man's fingers tightened on Tyler's hair, making his scalp sting as Jace held him in place. "Fuck," Jace said, sounding pained. "Now I'm uncomfortably turned on. You're right. We have to stop." Even as Jace made the claim, he nibbled on Tyler's bottom lip.

"Jesus, Jace. I'm convinced you're fucking perfect. Can I keep you?"

Jace pulled away at the question. "What?"

Tyler smiled at the adorable confusion etching Jace's features. "I want to be with you," he said, trying a different track.

Jace's expression didn't clear.

A chuckle escaped Tyler. "I'm trying not to sound like I'm twelve while asking you to be my boyfriend."

A smile exploded across Jace's face. "What? No paper for me to check yes or no?"

"I could find one," Tyler said, one hundred percent serious.

"Are we finishing this sometime tonight? I need to be on the road by five in the morning," Adam said behind them.

Jace laughed as he stepped away from Tyler and headed for the back door. Tyler was hot on his heels, opening the door for him before Jace could do it for himself. "So you're just going to leave me hanging here?" Tyler asked as they headed down the hall for Adam's bedroom.

Jace didn't look at him again until after he grabbed a laundry basket filled with clothes. "I check yes," he said, sweeping past Tyler as if he hadn't changed everything between them.

"Does that mean I can stay the night?"

Jace tossed a wink over his shoulder. "You're more than welcome to stay on the couch."

The game was on. So be it. Tyler would do whatever it took.

*

Jace's face hurt from smiling. The stupid grin stretching his lips hadn't slipped since Tyler asked to stay. Perhaps he'd enjoyed handing Tyler a pillow and blanket for his night on the couch a little too much. Now he stared at the darkened ceiling of his bedroom, worrying over the way Tyler's feet hung over the edge of the sofa. Jace's stomach muscles were tight with anticipation. Every creak of the house settling had Jace straining to hear if it was Tyler coming down the hall. Why was he doing this again? After twenty minutes of hoping Tyler would break the rules, Jace wondered who he was punishing.

Jace made it forty-five minutes before he was out of bed. He'd just check on Tyler. After all, the man was way too tall for Jace's couch. If Tyler was sleeping, Jace would head back to bed—no guilt.

Tyler's deep voice rumbled through the darkness. "Is everything okay?"

Instead of answering, Jace kept moving until he reached Tyler's side. He held his hand out for Tyler. "Come on, babe. You've got to work tomorrow and your back will be killing you all day if you stay out here."

Tyler grabbed his pillow and accepted Jace's hand. "If that's what you want."

Jace padded back to the bedroom with Tyler in tow. At the edge of the bed, Jace stripped down to his underwear and climbed in. Tyler set one knee on the bed, still wearing his pants.

A laugh escaped Jace. "You don't have to leave your pants on."

Taking him at his word, Tyler dropped his pants on the floor before crawling in next to Jace. "Should we build a pillow wall?" Tyler asked with laughter lacing his words.

"That's going to make it hard for you to hold me." Jace slid closer as he made the claim. Tyler didn't hesitate to open his arms for Jace. A deep sigh rose in Jace's throat the instant his head hit Tyler's chest. The man's heartbeat thumped against Jace's ear. It was the most soothing sound Jace had ever heard. He couldn't stop rubbing Tyler's stomach. It felt so soft beneath Jace's palm. Tyler didn't complain. Jace's hand slid lower. Tyler's fingertips traced a pattern down the back of Jace's arm. While holding his breath, Jace dipped one finger beneath the band of Tyler's underwear. He ran his finger along Tyler's skin beneath the band. Still no protest came from Tyler. Jace dove in, finding Tyler hard. He palmed Tyler's erection. Silky skin over hardened steel tempted Jace's touch. Tyler's breath hitched. Jace felt it against his ear. He bit back a smile as he slipped lower. The rough hair covering Tyler's balls scraped the tips of Jace's fingers. Jace lightly traced the thick veins in Tyler's dick. Moisture touched Jace's wrist, letting him know Tyler's cock leaked from Jace's touch. Jace couldn't remember the last time he felt so empowered. The way Tyler struggled for air made Jace bolder. He fisted Tyler's dick. His own cock soaked the front of his underwear in response.

Tyler tolerated Jace for three strokes before drawing Jace's hand away and holding it to his chest. "You're making it real hard for me to pass your test."

As much as Jace wanted to deny this was a test, he couldn't. Instead, he chose a different argument. "You passed when you stayed on the couch."

Tyler's lips touched Jace's temple. "Baby, you need to see I want to be with you without sex. I want to show you it's you I care about. Not what I can get from you. I want you to trust me."

The honesty in Tyler's voice not only had Jace's throat swelling, it also had Jace giving Tyler the truth. "I've never been more terrified."

At the confession, Tyler rolled to his side, coming face to face with Jace. Tyler's eyes sparkled in the dark. Jace could feel his interest, so he kept baring his soul. "The desire to feel your skin against mine is crippling, but what if you don't call again afterward?"

"You're proving my point," Tyler said. "I want you to be ready and know in your heart I'm always coming back. You don't believe in me yet. I need you to believe in me."

Without thought, Jace's fingers skimmed Tyler's stomach. It was as if he couldn't get enough of touching Tyler—

108

like he already trusted the man to keep him safe from his fears. "I don't think this choking fear will ever go away until you make love to me and don't disappear afterward."

"I won't disappear," Tyler said as he slowly leaned in. "You can stop me anytime. I won't be mad," Tyler whispered. His lips barely brushed Jace's with the final word.

Jace held still, waiting for Tyler's next move. Their lips clung. With the slightest urging, Jace's mouth opened for Tyler's kiss as Tyler coaxed Jace onto his back. Tyler's body covered Jace's. He'd never experienced anything as sweet. It was like Tyler was taking him to the letter of his word, making love to him. Jace didn't think anyone had ever been so soft with him. The man's slow movements gave Jace the freedom to enjoy every sensation. The inside of his knee brushed the outside of

Tyler's hip as he lifted his leg. The base of his spine itched at the contact. Tyler's short nails scraped Jace's hip as he peeled Jace's underwear from his body. Jace dutifully lifted his hips and let Tyler have the piece of clothing.

"I hope you have a condom around here."

"Top drawer in the bathroom."

At Jace's answer, Tyler slipped from the bed and headed for the bathroom. Jace tried not to squirm under the pressure of waiting for Tyler's return. Tyler reappeared suited up and with a bottle of lube. Jace tried catching his breath without much luck. He heard the tube open and snap closed again before Tyler tossed it aside. Jace's knees fell open as Tyler crawled between them. His lubed fingers stretched Jace's asshole. Jace shamelessly rode the man's hand. Pops of electricity caused his cock to twitch against his stomach. Jace had never been so attuned to every sensation.

"You're still free to stop me, Jace. Even if I'm inside you and you don't want me anymore, I'll stop and still come back tomorrow. And the next day," Tyler added as he settled between Jace's thighs. "And the day after that," he said as he positioned his thick crown against Jace's asshole.

Jace gasped as Tyler pushed past the tight ring of muscles and sank inside him.

Tyler's body molded to Jace's, and still Tyler's promises kept coming. "In fact, I don't think I can stay away ever again. You'll have to be the one to tell me to go away."

Before Jace had time to say he didn't have any such intentions, Tyler's mouth covered Jace's. Their tongues clashed. Tyler rocked forward. The motion was slow. Torturous. Jace never wanted him to

111

stop. With his weight braced on one arm, Tyler moved inside Jace while palming Jace's cock. Their lips met, clung, and retreated before repeating the pattern. They shared each other's oxygen. It was a meeting of the souls. Jace's eyes stung from the sweetness of the moment. He'd never felt more cherished. This man, he was every dream Jace had ever had. Tyler could destroy him. For Jace, the reward outweighed the risk. If his heart was destined to be crushed, Jace couldn't ask for a better man to do it. He'd have this. Jace would always have this. All thought fled as his body braced for orgasm.

"So beautiful," Tyler whispered. "So perfect."

Jace's slow burn became an inferno. A silent scream tore from his throat as an orgasm tore through him.

"My baby," Tyler said as he captured Jace's mouth, seeming to savor the flood of cum squishing between them as he fucked Jace's ass. Tiny noises vibrated around their entwined tongues as Tyler came. With every whimper, Tyler stole another piece of Jace. Even as they curled into each other's arms and drifted off to sleep, Jace accepted the truth. He'd never find anyone like Tyler again.

Chapter 4

Jace hadn't woken up in Tyler's arms as he'd hoped. What he got was just as nice—Tyler had been awake, making breakfast with Adam. Together, they'd seen Adam off. Jace had never been more grateful for anyone's company as he had been Tyler's. He hadn't expected Adam's parting to hit him the way it had, but damn. Jace would miss Adam. His house was like a tomb now.

Thankfully, Tyler kept showing up every night the minute he got off work. They ate together. Tyler took him to see where he lived and worked, in case Jace ever needed to find him for anything. They slept next to each other each night. It was nice. Every text, phone call, and visit had Jace feeling more and more secure in what they had. One thing he knew for certain, no one had ever made him feel the way Tyler did. Jace didn't want it to stop.

There were flowers waiting for him when he returned from going to lunch with Paige. He knew right away something was up by the way the receptionist kept trying to rush him back to his exam room. As soon as he spotted the vase overflowing with blooms, Jace's heart had skipped a beat before racing to life again. They were lilies. Jace's favorite. Since he'd never said as much, Jace's smile grew to unrealistic proportions as he read the card attached.

I almost sent roses, but they seemed too cliché. How ridiculous is it that I miss you already?

–Tyler

"Is he cheating on you already?"

Jace hid his instant outrage behind a scoff. "What the hell kind of question is that, Paige?"

After tossing her brown hair over one shoulder, Paige shrugged. "Only cheaters send flowers. Men never do anything nice like that otherwise."

"Okay," Jace said, drawing out the word. "Well, until Tyler proves to be one of those people, I'll enjoy my moment of happiness. I don't get them very often."

Paige's face fell. "I'm sorry, Jace. You know I'm just stressed out because Anthony hasn't called."

Jace nodded while trying to listen as she ran through the entire story of how she'd met some guy on a dating app, slept with him, and now was shocked he hadn't called or returned any of her messages. Honestly, Jace understood her rage. It was more that she'd told him the story already. Four times. He nodded, listening to it a fifth, because that's what friends did. Jace already knew she didn't need his input. As long as he nodded, she was fine to carry on with her rant, whether he was really listening or not. Generally, he always tried to care about Paige's problems. Jace knew from experience that she didn't want to hear his opinion.

When he hit a point where he couldn't listen to another word, Jace made his excuses before sneaking into the supply closet to text Tyler.

Jace: *I love the flowers. Thank you.*

Tyler: *Would roses have been better? I've second-guessed myself all day.*

Jace: *No. Lilies are my favorite. They're beautiful.*

Tyler: *I'm glad you like them. Missing you like crazy, in case you didn't notice.*

Jace's fingers hovered over the buttons. As hard as he tried not to let Paige get in his head, it seemed she always knew what to say to make him question everything good.

Jace: *Paige said only cheaters send flowers. LOL!*

He couldn't help adding the laugh out loud, so—hopefully—he wouldn't sound like he was questioning Tyler's motives.

Tyler: *I wouldn't know since I've never sent anyone flowers before, and I'm definitely no cheat. Sounds like she's still mad at me if she'd say something like that and ruin your present.*

He had a point. Maybe Paige was still harboring some anger toward Tyler. After all, she wasn't as forgiving of a person as Jace.

Jace: *Nothing could ruin this present. In*

fact, I think a gift such as this deserves a reward.

Tyler: *I'm listening...*

Jace: *Nope. You have to come over tonight and find out for yourself.*

Tyler: *I'm there. Have a good day, baby.*

He loved when Tyler called him "baby." Jace stared at his phone, reading Tyler's message several times before responding.

Jace: *You too.*

The rest of the day slowed to a crawl as Jace waited for the moment he'd be with Tyler again. A part of him wanted to kick himself for allowing his mood to revolve around seeing Tyler. The rest of Jace kept telling that small part to fuck off. Tyler was everything Jace had been looking for so long now. He wouldn't screw this up by overthinking things.

He ran by the grocery store on the way home and grabbed everything needed to make Tyler a nice dinner. It wasn't a spectacular surprise or anything, but he hoped Tyler would see it for the gesture it was meant to be. Jace knew he worked hard and wanted to take care of him. Jace turned on the TV in the kitchen as he washed the vegetables for their salad. The news caught his eye.

"Olivia Lucas, the seven-year-old girl who went missing last Wednesday after getting off the school bus, has been found dead."

Jace switched off the water in the kitchen sink and focused all his attention on the TV. Like everyone, he'd been following the story of the missing girl. Her poor parents. He couldn't imagine. Jace listened as they recapped the story of her disappearance as well as the search party's efforts afterward. Tyler's image appeared on the screen. Jace's heart fell. He turned the volume up and moved closer.

"We caught up with the detective in charge of Olivia's case a few minutes ago. Here's what he had to say." The images shifted and the blonde reporter held her microphone under Tyler's nose. "Thank you for taking a few minutes to talk to us, Detective. Is there anything more you can tell us about the circumstances surrounding Olivia's death?"

Tyler didn't look like himself. His eyes were dead. Jace felt sick. "We're still processing the evidence. It's too early to release any information. The chief of police has a press conference scheduled for later tonight. Hopefully, we'll have more information for you then."

Jace barely stopped himself from

calling Tyler right then. Only the knowledge Tyler had his hands full stopped him. He wanted to offer what comfort he could. Jace spent fifteen minutes debating before finally texting him.

Jace: *Saw the news. I'm SO sorry. Tell me what I can do?*

Tyler: *Seeing your name on my phone helped. I don't think I'll make it by tonight.*

Jace: *It's fine. Do what you need to do. You know where I am when you're free. I knew your job was unpredictable from the start. Don't worry over me.*

Tyler: *I'll make it up to you.*

Jace: *You have bigger things to deal with right now. {{HUGS}} I'll be here when you're done.*

Tyler: *Okay. **hugs back***

Jace felt a little better after reading Tyler's texts. Still, there was a nagging feeling way down in his gut—one he couldn't place. He couldn't imagine how anyone could see the things Tyler did and stay sane. Jace was almost scared of what he'd see in the man's eyes when he saw him next. Jace's phone buzzed again, startling him. He glanced down, expecting Tyler. A spurt of disappointment hit when it wasn't him.

Paige: *I saw Tyler on the news. That's awful.*

Jace: *Yeah. My heart is breaking for him.*

Paige: *I'm sure he's already using this an excuse not to see you for a while.*

Jace: *I knew his job would keep him away sometimes when I chose to date him. It's fine.*

Paige: *If you say so.*

* * *

As Tyler predicted, he didn't make it to see Jace after Jace saw him on the news. Since Jace had known the man was busy,

123

he didn't let it bother him until day three of not hearing a word had come and gone. He knew there was something more to Tyler's no-show status. By the end of the fourth day with no word from Tyler, Jace broke. He'd already been on edge, imagining what Tyler must be going through while working that little girl's case. The not speaking was driving him insane. He finally texted him.

Jace: *Are you still kicking?*

Thankfully, for his sanity's sake, he heard back almost immediately.

Tyler: *Yes. Sorry. I'm about ten minutes from my house. I plan to grab a shower and snack before heading back in to work.*

Jace: *Okay. Just wanted to check.*

Tyler: *I really am sorry. Guess I should've warned you my job can be like this. Miss you.*

For Jace, Tyler admitting he missed him was everything. As long as he had that, and the knowledge Tyler's job was an important one, he could deal.

Jace: *Stop apologizing. I miss you too.*

Tyler: *First chance I get, I'm making this up to you. You won't regret keeping me.*

Jace: *Although I'm already tingling with the need to see what you'll do, I also have to say being with you is no burden. Just text me once in a while so I know you're still breathing.*

Tyler: *I like it when you tingle.*

Jace chewed his bottom lip. The more he heard from Tyler, the more Jace wanted. He said he didn't mind, and he didn't, but the desire to set eyes on the man ate at Jace's gut. Before he could change his mind, Jace grabbed his keys and headed for the door. Tyler only lived a few minutes' drive away and there was a coffee shop between here and there. He could stop and grab the man some caffeine to keep him going, steal a few precious moments with him, and then Jace could be on his way. Surely that wasn't too pushy.

Despite all his internal pep talks, doubt set in as Jace pulled into the driveway of Tyler's single-family brick home. The place was dark, and the grass needed mowing. Jace focused on the mundane, hoping to keep his nervousness at bay. Tyler's police-issue Buick sat in the driveway. The way it popped and hissed said Tyler hadn't been home long. Jace hoped this wasn't a mistake. Tyler's mood could be anything, considering the stress of the last few days. Even after he knocked on the front door, Jace questioned his decision to come here. The door swung open. Jace's heart squeezed in his chest. Tyler's hair stood in every direction. He had dark circles under his eyes and looked as if he wore the same clothes as he had the last time Jace had seen him, making

Jace wonder if this was the first time the man had been home in days.

Jace held up the coffee and bag of donuts. "I'm doing my part to keep you moving."

Tyler's mouth lifted in one corner. "Damn," he breathed, making Jace's stomach cramp with desire. "You're amazing." Tyler stepped back, inviting Jace inside.

Jace's steps faltered as he crossed the threshold. Crime scene photos were scattered around the room as if Tyler had created a mirror image of the actual scene in his house to study.

"Shit," Tyler cursed, rushing to gather the photos. "I wasn't thinking."

Jace wanted to tell Tyler it was okay. The words wouldn't come. Even with Tyler snatching up the worst of the pictures, Jace had seen more than he cared to ever see again. His heart was breaking.

127

"She was someone's child," Jace said without thought. "I mean, everyone is, but she was so young. What you do is really horrific." He was making things worse. Jace could feel it, but he wasn't expressing himself the way he wanted.

"Thanks for the coffee," Tyler said, sounding disappointed as he reached for the cup.

Jace refused to release it, forcing Tyler to meet his gaze. "I've never been prouder of anyone in my life than I am of you right now."

They stood, both holding the cup as if suspended in time as they stared at each other. Tyler looked as if he held his breath. "The world needs more people like you. People willing to help little humans who need justice. You're amazing." Jace didn't know if he was getting his point across, but the words needed saying. Tyler did something no one should have to do because someone needed to do it. His job was too important for everyone to be too chicken-shit to handle it.

Tyler relieved Jace of the cup and bag. He set them aside. Without a word, he dragged Jace into his arms and captured his lips. Jace swore he could feel Tyler's heart in their kiss — the man's pain. He wouldn't talk to Jace about the past few days. Jace already knew it, but Jace could bring him comfort in other ways.

"Goddamn, take this off," Tyler begged, tugging at Jace's shirt.

Jace didn't hesitate. After tugging the shirt over his head, he tossed it aside. Tyler came back for more. "Swear I'm not taking advantage," he said between kisses. "Just want to feel your skin." Jace didn't care what Tyler's reasons were. He wished the man would take advantage. If he needed comfort, Jace was willing. The desperation in Tyler's kiss made Jace want to fix it. The first button on Tyler's shirt came loose between Jace's fingers without any argument from Tyler. Jace moved to the second. He trailed his lips down Tyler's neck to his chest, enjoying the skin he'd bared.

"Damn, Jace. I can't even remember the last time I showered."

Still, Tyler wasn't stopping him, so Jace continued to undress him. With the man's shirt unbuttoned. Jace left it hanging open and went for the pants. This wasn't about sex, even though Jace's erection had other thoughts on the matter. The instant he had Tyler's pants open, he shoved his hand inside and palmed Tyler's cock.

"When do you need to be back at work?"

A pant escaped Tyler. "Um. Not until tomorrow really. I was just headed back tonight because... damn. I'm not sure," he said, moving against Jace's palm. Tyler forced Jace's chin up and claimed his mouth. The man's chest heaved with every indrawn breath as Jace stroked. He handled Tyler's cock as he would his, intent on quick results. Tyler bit Jace's bottom lip, making him gasp at the sharp pain. He sucked on it as if apologizing. Jace's dick beat against the inside of his zipper, as if jealous of Jace's bottom lip. Jace pressed his thumb against Tyler's slit, enjoying the pre-cum wetting his fingers as he pumped. The way Tyler openly fucked Jace's fist had Jace ready to come in his jeans. The man was so damn sexual, and the way he owned it made Jace horny as hell.

Tyler's body tensed. Jace tightened his hold and quickened his pace. Hot semen hit Jace's stomach and chest in streams. The pressure tightening Jace's balls threatened to blow at the way Tyler moaned against Jace's mouth. This man, he made Jace feel so goddamn powerful.

Tyler's kiss moved from Jace's lips to his chin before licking a path down Jace's neck. "See? I knew you needed to lose the shirt for a reason," he said against Jace's collarbone. Jace chuckled as he tilted his head back, giving Tyler better access to anything he wanted. When Tyler's tongue curled around Jace's nipple, Jace's fingers found the man's hair and held on. As his lips moved lower, Jace's dick danced with joy. Tyler made a humming noise against Jace's skin as he licked away the mess he'd made.

Jace's chin hit his chest. He had to see it happen. This man hadn't been lying. He was kinky as fuck and Jace loved it. Never had anyone made him want to come just by watching them in action. Seeing Tyler licking away his own cum from Jace's stomach was the hottest thing Jace had ever witnessed. Jace's stomach caved as Tyler reached the edge of Jace's jeans. It was as if his body hinted Tyler should dip inside the material. Tyler didn't hesitate before ripping open Jace's zipper. He fell to his knees, met Jace's stare, and slowly opened his mouth around Jace's hard dick.

Jace's breath caught in his throat. He locked his knees to keep from going down. This man owned him. Tyler never broke eye contact as he took Jace down his throat. Jace brushed his fingers through Tyler's hair and rubbed his palm over Tyler's beard. He touched Tyler every place he could reach, silently praising the man's efforts.

Tyler dragged Jace's jeans lower until he could play with Jace's balls. Jace knew he wouldn't last long. Tyler liked it too much. This wasn't a blowjob. This was Tyler, feasting on Jace's body. No man could withstand that type of treatment.

"You're so fucking sexy," Jace praised when he realized he'd been staring intently for way too long. "You make me wonder where I went right in life." Jace blew out a breath, trying not to come too fast. He enjoyed seeing Tyler on his knees, but he'd gotten too worked up while handling Tyler's cock. While grinding his back teeth, Jace drew several slow breaths through his nose. It wasn't helping. Pressure beat at his crown. He wanted the explosion. The blinding ecstasy at Tyler's hands. A gasp left him as the first wave hit. Tyler hollowed his cheeks and sucked harder. His eyes fell closed. His look of pure delight had Jace forcing his eyes to remain open even as his body shook from the pleasure. Tyler's fingers dug into Jace's ass cheeks, as if doing his part to keep Jace upright as he drained Jace.

Tyler buried his face against Jace's

stomach and sucked air, as if he'd ran for miles. "Thank you," he whispered against Jace's skin. Jace ran his hands through Tyler's hair, unsure of what he'd done to earn Tyler's gratitude. Tyler pushed to his feet and snagged Jace's hand. "Come on." He headed for the hall.

"Where are we going?"

Tyler glanced over his shoulder. "First, we're taking a long, hot shower together and then we're going to bed. I'm not finished with you yet."

Jace smiled so hard his face hurt as he allowed Tyler to lead him down the hall. He'd been to Tyler's house once before, but only long enough for Tyler to change clothes before they went to dinner. He'd never ventured into Tyler's bedroom. Jace was ridiculously curious. Tyler's house was sparse, as if he barely spent any time there. It gave no insight to the man.

Tyler didn't bother with the lights

when they reached his bedroom. Jace barely caught a glimpse of the room before Tyler led him inside the bathroom. When the lights flared to life, Jace winced against the sudden assault on his vision. As Tyler fired up the shower, Jace caught a glimpse of himself in the mirror. His lips were swollen from Tyler's kisses, a flush rode high on his cheeks, and there was beard burn on his neck. He looked happy. Jace couldn't tear his gaze away from the sight. When was the last time he'd felt anything other than disdain for life? He couldn't remember.

Jace's eyes fell closed as Tyler's arms encircled his waist, drawing Jace back against his chest. Tyler's hand slid up Jace's chest until he reached Jace's jaw. He urged Jace's head back onto his shoulder and captured his mouth. It was an awkward position for a kiss, but Jace didn't care. Any time Tyler's tongue entwined with his, Jace forgot everything—where they were... his name. The air thickened with steam. Tyler's teeth sank into Jace's bottom lip, drawing it between his lips for the man to suck. His hold tightened on Jace.

"You have no idea how much I needed this tonight."

Jace's heart skipped a beat at Tyler's confession. Tyler made him sound important. He was scared to hope. "I needed it too. For the past few days, I've been pacing the floor, worrying about you."

"You should've called."

"I didn't want to bother you," Jace said, admitting something he hadn't wanted to confess.

Tyler held Jace's chin, forcing Jace to meet his gaze. "I am never too busy to hear from you. This is a real relationship, Jace. I'm not killing time until someone better comes along. There's no one better. You're it. Call next time."

Jace nodded because his tongue wouldn't work. Tyler's "you're it" sounded a lot like "you're the one" and Jace was scared shitless by how badly he wanted that to be true.

* * *

Tyler: *How about I pick you up from work when you get off, and we'll go out to dinner?*

Jace: *Sounds great. I'm ready to see you.*

"What's got you smiling?"

Jace blushed at Paige's question. He flashed his phone Paige's way. "Nothing really. Tyler's coming to get me so we can go out to eat."

"Awww, that's sweet. I wonder why he never wants you to pick him up?"

Jace's face screwed up in confusion. He felt it happen. "What do you mean? He gets off before me."

Paige shrugged as if she hadn't meant anything at all. "I was just thinking out loud. You know how these alpha male types are. They don't always want anyone knowing they're gay, and he's a cop. I just wonder if he doesn't want you showing up at his work."

It was obvious Paige wasn't trying to hurt his feelings, but she had. He shrugged, trying not to show it. "Like I said, he gets off before me. Besides, even if he doesn't want anyone he works with to know about me, I don't care. All I care about is how he treats me, and he's damn good to me."

Paige's smile grew. "I'm so glad to hear that. Well, I'm out of here. That was your last patient for the day. If I leave now, I can get my nails done." She waved her already perfectly manicured nails Jace's way. He laughed because he knew that was what

Paige expected. With a final wave of her fingers, Paige disappeared. Jace made it ten minutes before deciding that since he was done for the day, he'd pick Tyler up at work.

Jace cursed himself all through the fifteen-minute drive. Every time he thought he felt secure in their relationship, something happened to make him question another aspect. The thing was, now that he was headed to Tyler's work, he couldn't understand why. Of course, even knowing he was being an idiot didn't stop Jace from walking inside the building. The nondescript red brick building was every bit as unassuming on the inside. There was nothing more than a medium-sized room with a man behind bulletproof glass. He stepped up to the glass.

"I'm here to see Detective Tyler Phillips."

The man nodded. "Take a seat. I'll let him know you're here."

Jace glanced behind him. Sure enough, there was one small metal chair against the wall. Jace sat. The chair was cold. In fact, the whole damn experience was uncomfortable. Tyler worked here every day. How depressing. After several minutes, Tyler finally appeared through a door Jace hadn't even noticed, it blended so well with the off-white walls. His expression went from questioning to ecstatic in an instant. Jace's insides shook as he came to his feet. He hadn't realized until that moment how important Tyler's reaction was to him.

"I thought I was picking you up," Tyler said as he crossed the room.

Jace wiped his hands on his thighs. "My last appointment of the day was thirty minutes ago, so I thought I'd pick you up for a change." To his surprise, Tyler captured his lips in a hot kiss. The shaking in Jace's stomach increased. He never expected to meet this amazing man. Now, he'd never been more terrified to lose anyone.

Chapter 5

"You have a visitor out front."

Tyler glanced up from the reports he was finishing and focused on the cop hovering over his desk. Dan had twenty years on Tyler. Unfortunately, that age gap brought with it some old-school beliefs. Judging by his disapproving stare, Tyler could guess who was here. A smile he couldn't control pulled at the corners of his mouth. Tyler stood and pushed his chair in.

"Thanks for letting me know, Dan," Tyler said, refusing to let the man's hate bring him down. A little of Jace was exactly what Tyler needed right now. He moved faster than necessary toward the front lobby. His steps faltered when he caught sight of Jimmy. His brows drew together in his confusion. Tyler wasn't disappointed, per se, even though he would've loved to have seen Jace, it was more that Jimmy was the last person in the world Tyler expected.

"Hey."

Jimmy didn't smile. He gave a jerky nod. "Hey."

"What brings you by?" Tyler asked, trying to keep from sounding as surprised as he felt.

"Eli made me." Before Tyler had time to get his feelings hurt, Jimmy sighed and added, "That's not entirely true."

"Okay." Tyler dragged the word out, not bothering to hide his confusion.

Jimmy shifted from one foot to the other. His gaze bounced around the room, looking everywhere but at Tyler. He looked cagey as hell. Tyler would've shaken him if he wasn't one hundred percent certain Jimmy could and would hand his ass to him. "Um." Jimmy pulled his hair up into a bun. It was a nervous gesture he'd seen the man do a thousand times. Tyler held on to his patience. Dealing with Jimmy always took every ounce of his training. "Here's the thing," Jimmy said, finally meeting Tyler's stare. "You're all the family I've got, and Eli doesn't have anyone. We're asking a lot, because we decided to get married in Miami, on the beach, before flying out the next day for our honeymoon. I get that it's super-inconvenient, but you know how Eli is with crowds, and a regular wedding just won't be comfortable for him with everyone staring at him. So a beach wedding is definitely the way to go."

"That's awesome," Tyler said, wondering where this was headed.

Jimmy nodded. "We were wondering if you'd like to stand up with us, like giving us away or being our witness or some shit. You know, it's okay if you can't. It's short notice and not a big deal at all."

Tyler couldn't believe his ears. He

didn't know if he was more shocked by Jimmy's question or his rambling. "It is a big deal. When is this thing happening?"

"Two weeks from tomorrow."

Jimmy chewed his bottom lip while Tyler thought things over. It was short notice, but he had some vacation time plus seniority. He could swing it. "I'm there. Just get me the details, so I can get my trip booked." Another thought hit. "I realize it may be awkward, since Jace is your ex and all, but is it okay if he comes with me?"

A smile exploded across Jimmy's face, taking Tyler aback. It was the first time he'd seen Jimmy smile when Eli wasn't around. Not the first time in a long time. The first time ever. When it came to him, Jimmy didn't smile. Tyler got it. He reminded Jimmy of something ugly— something he wanted to forget. Still, Tyler's throat swelled at the sight. For a moment, Tyler felt as if he'd accomplished something. He hadn't completely failed Jimmy in this life. He hadn't failed every child he'd tried to help.

"Eli's at Jace's work as we speak, hoping to enlist him in stealing you away for that weekend if you turned me down."

Even as a smile pulled at the corners of Tyler's mouth, Jimmy's words stung a bit. "Did you really think I'd turn you down?"

Jimmy shrugged. His smile slipped away. "It's not like you owe me anything. I'm just some kid you took in because no one else could be bothered."

The swelling in Tyler's throat increased. "That's not true, Jimmy. You've always been more than that to me."

Jimmy's gaze bounced away again. He cleared his throat. "So I can tell Eli you said yes?"

Tyler recognized he'd gotten all he'd get

from Jimmy today. He slapped the man across the shoulder. "Hell yeah. I'm there. Someone's tying you down? I'm not missing that for the world." His phone buzzed in his front pocket. "Excuse me," Tyler said, digging out his phone.

Jace: *Are you going?*

"It's Jace," he explained without looking up. "Guess Eli has already spoken with him."

"Is he going?"

Tyler sent Jace a message while he answered Jimmy. "Hold on. I'll find out."

Tyler: *Are you going with me?*

Jace: *I feel weird about it.*

"He says he feels weird about it."

Jimmy sighed. "Call him."

Tyler knew that tone. He smiled as he dialed Jace's number. When Jace answered, Tyler didn't bother saying hello. "Jimmy wants to talk to you." He passed the phone Jimmy's way and held his breath, hoping Jace didn't hang up on him.

Jimmy pressed the device to his ear. "Quit being a pussy," Jimmy said, not bothering to sugarcoat anything. "Tyler wants you there. As far as I know, he's never let anyone else into his life to the level he has with you, so man the fuck up and pack a bag."

Although Tyler couldn't make out what Jace was saying, he heard the man talking a mile a minute, letting him know Jace was giving Jimmy hell. To his surprise, Jimmy smiled as he listened. "For real, I think Tyler loves you," Jimmy said when Jace took a breath. Tyler blinked. Surely he hadn't heard Jimmy right. No sound came from the phone. Either Jace had dropped his voice, or he was every bit as speechless as Tyler. "Is Eli still there? Put my baby on the phone."

Tyler shook off his shock. "Wait. No

149

phone sex on my phone."

Jimmy's expression turned sullen. "Fine. Tell my baby to get out of sight and answer his phone. I have some things I need to tell him." Tyler's eyebrows hit his hairline at the sex dripping from Jimmy's words. Wow. He'd definitely never seen this side of the man.

"Don't hang up," Tyler said before Jimmy did just that. "I want to talk to my baby too," he added with a wink.

Jimmy nodded. "Here's Tyler." He handed the phone back to Tyler. "I'll text you all the details," Jimmy said before turning to walk away. "See you in Miami," he called over his shoulder.

With a shake of his head, Tyler pressed the device to his ear. "You still there?"

"Yeah."

"Has Eli left yet?"

"Yeah, he left as soon as I told him Jimmy was about to call him."

Tyler's smile grew with every word. Jace sounded flustered. That meant Tyler had him right where he wanted him. "So you going with?"

"Seems so—not that I needed Jimmy's lecture. I'd already gotten one hell of a guilt trip from Eli before you called."

"Cool. I plan to add to it."

"That's not nice," Jace grumbled.

Tyler talked over the top of him. "I was thinking—I haven't had a real vacation in years. How do you feel about heading to Miami a few days early and relaxing on the beach?"

The line went quiet. For a moment, Tyler wondered if Jace had hung up on him before he spoke again. "It depends. I'll have to either clear my appointments or call in another hygienist from a different location. If I can pull it off, then I'd love to."

Tyler was smiling like an idiot. There was no calling it under control. "Let me

151

know. I'll go ahead and put in for a vacation. If you can't get free those days, I'll just dog your heels instead."

"Fantastic."

He got the impression Jace meant to be sarcastic, but the word came out sounding breathless instead. "You should come over tonight and let me make you dinner."

"I have a fight scheduled."

Jace's tone was full of regret, but Tyler couldn't have been more thrilled. "Seriously? Can I watch?"

A nervous-sounding chuckle rang through the line. "I suppose. It's at Smith Brothers at eight. The place gets kind of crowded pretty fast. You can go with me, but I have to be there by six or you can show up about half-an-hour early and circle the block until you can get a parking space."

"Hmmm," Tyler said, making as if he

needed to think it over. "Let's see. So my choices are either I can spend more time with you or I can drive around all night hunting for a parking space. Damn. Guess I'm stuck with you for a couple of extra hours. The sacrifices I make for this relationship."

"I know," Jace said. His voice had gone husky. "Maybe if I don't get my ass handed to me too badly, I can make it up to you later."

Tyler glanced around, looking for a place to hide before everyone in the front lobby saw him go hard. Checking his pocket, he ensured he had his keys before heading for the car. "How many people are looking at you right now?"

"None. I hid in the supply closet the minute Eli left," Jace said on a low laugh.

Tyler waited until he was alone inside his car—out of sight and earshot of anyone—before responding. "Damn. Now you've got me wondering what I can convince you to do."

"Uh, nothing," Jace said immediately. "I said I was hiding, but I should've added 'out of hearing range.' People are in and out of here all day. I'm not getting fired and having 'got caught jacking-off at work' stamped on my employment record for the rest of my life."

At the heavy laughter in Jace's voice, Tyler relaxed in his seat. He could easily talk to Jace all day. Tyler loved the sound of his voice. "No. I'm not trying to get you fired. How about you tell me about your day?"

"If you'd like."

"I would," Tyler said, leaning his head back against the headrest.

"Okay. After I left your house, I got stuck in traffic on Broad. No idea why. Somehow, I made it to work on time, even though I didn't try." The laughter in Jace's every word had a stupid grin stretching Tyler's lips. He wanted every piece of Jace. "I've already seen seven patients this morning, and it hasn't slowed. Paige keeps trying to corner me to talk about this guy she met online. Scary thought there, but wow. My life sounds way more drab when I say it out loud."

"I'm not the least bit bored. Want to hear about my day so far?"

"Absolutely," Jace said, doing nothing to dim Tyler's smile.

"I've filled out reports. All day long. So many fucking reports, it's all just running together in my head. Now that's the most mundane shit ever, but that's okay. My job is only exciting when bad things happen. I'll happily accept dull over that. Is it stupid I want to leave work right now and come sit with you while you work?"

"Is that your way of saying you miss me?"

Tyler had no shame when it came to Jace. "So much."

He could hear the smile in Jace's voice when he responded. "Then no, it's not stupid at all. I miss you too."

An idea hit. "What time do you go to lunch?"

"I have one more patient before then, so maybe thirty minutes."

Tyler checked his watch. "Would you like to have lunch with me?"

"Sounds great."

His happiness level was off the charts when it came to Jace. "Awesome. I'll pick you up in half an hour."

"Okay. See ya then."

"Yeah. See ya." Tyler hung up before he made an idiot of himself. He also wanted Jace to get that last patient out of the way since he had no intention of heading back inside. Instead, he called in his break and headed Jace's way. He was ridiculously excited to see a man he'd seen less than five hours earlier. Tyler was so fucked. He'd never had it this bad.

*

Jace tried his best not to rush through the next cleaning. Paige kept shooting him dirty looks. She'd hoped he would join her for lunch so she could tell him all about her new man. He'd been forced to promise to buy her lunch tomorrow to keep from enduring her wrath. Tyler was worth it. Jace couldn't explain the way he felt. He'd never missed anyone after only a few short hours. Jace had also never had anyone long to be with him the way Tyler did. It was addicting.

Paige tried for one last dig before Jace left. "All you care about is Tyler these days. He gets you all the time. It's almost like he's trying to separate you from your friends."

"Wow, Paige. It's one lunch. I get seven

157

of those a week." Despite the humor in his voice, Jace was a step beyond irritated. He never said things like that to Paige. If the shoe was on the other foot, he'd be happy for her.

"It's just one lunch today," Paige muttered under her breath as she walked away.

By the time Tyler's lips were brushing his, Jace felt like three hours had passed since their phone call rather than half an hour. The time they spent apart felt much longer than the moments they were together. Jace stared at Tyler's profile as he drove them to lunch. He didn't want to go back to work. In fact, Jace had never wanted to skip out on everything in his life that had meaning, like he had since meeting Tyler. All Jace cared to do any longer was crawl into the man's arms and try burrowing under his skin.

"How's Adam enjoying New York?"

Jace shrugged, even though Tyler was watching the road and not him. "He's getting to do what he loves, but I don't think it's as glamorous as he hoped."

"How so?"

"I gather his boss is a handful," Jace said, letting his humor over the matter slip through. "He's a harsh taskmaster, and as much as I love Adam, I can freely admit I also spoiled him. It seems this guy isn't as willing to give in to Adam's every whim."

A dimple appeared in Tyler's cheek. "Ah, life lessons. What about you? Has the empty-nest depression set in yet?"

Instead of answering, Jace chose to deflect. "Did you get like that after Jimmy left?"

"Of course," Tyler said without missing a beat and surprising Jace. "My job keeps me busy, and as you've seen, puts me in black, obsessive moods. All those things haven't exactly made me husband material. But I always wanted a real home with kids and someone who loves me," Tyler said, flashing Jace a quick smile. "I know I sound ridiculous, but that's what I've always wanted, and it didn't happen for me. Jimmy is what I got instead. So when he left, yeah, it made my house seem too empty."

"You could still have those things," Jace said, pointing out the facts.

Tyler scoffed. "I'm too old for all that now. Imagine my kid graduating from high school on the same day I file for social security."

Jace slapped his arm. "Don't say that. It makes me feel like I'm too old to have those things, and I've always hoped for them too."

"Hey," Tyler said, glancing over with his eyebrows raised. "Maybe Jimmy and Eli will adopt and we could spoil grandkids instead?"

Jace's stomach tied in knots at Tyler's words—like they had a real future together. Greed punched Jace in the gut. He craved the picture Tyler painted. "Let's hope not right away," Jace heard himself say. "I'm only thirty-three. That's too young to have anyone calling me grandpa."

"Huh," Tyler said as he pulled into The Sub Shoppe.

Jace had to know. "What's that 'huh' about?"

"It's just that I never expected to find anyone talking about being a grandpa hot. Say something else an old man would say and let's see if it was a fluke."

Jace's lips snapped into a smile. "In my day, we had to walk to school. Uphill both ways. In the snow."

"Holy fuck. That *was* hot," Tyler said, unsnapping his seatbelt and closing the distance between them. His mouth

161

covered Jace's. Jace's laughter died in his throat as Tyler's tongue brushed his.

Jace spoke against his lips. "Get off my lawn."

"So hard right now," Tyler said, coming at Jace from a different direction.

Jace shook with laughter, even as Tyler's teeth sank into Jace's bottom lip. "I can remember when gas was twenty-five cents." The words came out muffled around Tyler's kiss.

For a second, Tyler simply sucked on Jace's bottom lip. Jace's heart squeezed in his chest. Tyler was doing something to him. On the inside where no one could see. He was changing Jace, tying him in knots. Jace already didn't want to imagine a future without Tyler in it.

Tyler pulled away. His fingertips brushed Jace's jaw as he held his stare. "I love this."

"What?" The question came out in a

whisper. Jace was scared to break the spell.

"Being with you," Tyler said, causing Jace to lose his breath. "This happiness and laughter. I love it." Without another word, Tyler jumped from the car and circled around to Jace's side to help him from the car. Jace had no words. He loved it too.

Chapter 6

The weather was perfect in Miami—sunshine and warm breezes. The moment they were checked into their room, they wasted no time changing into their swim trunks and going on a tour of the resort. The first place they checked out was the spot where Jimmy and Eli would be married on Saturday. It was amazing. If it had been Eli's hope to have a peaceful ceremony, his wishes would soon come true. The spot was secluded from the rest of the property and had one hell of a view. Of course, Tyler had to concede part of the beach's charm for him might've been that Jace was standing on it.

He couldn't keep his thoughts to himself. "No one should be allowed to look as good as you do. Seriously, I'm afraid I might have to fight someone before the end of the weekend. All eyes follow you everywhere you go."

Jace scoffed. "Whatever. They're all drunk off the free drinks the resort is handing out." Before Tyler had time to argue, Jace pointed out a three-sided tent made up to look like a hut in the sand. "Hey, I think that's the relaxing spot to get a massage the concierge mentioned. We should check it out."

"If that's what you want," Tyler said, biting back the lecture he wanted to spew. It drove him bat-shit, trying to decide if Jace honestly didn't see himself the way Tyler did or if he didn't want to seem conceited. Either way, he made Tyler want to spank him.

As they approached the tent, a woman wearing a hotel uniform stepped out. She spotted them heading her way. "Are you coming in for a massage?"

"We're undecided," Jace answered for both of them.

Her brown hair shook as she tossed it over one shoulder. Her dark-brown gaze slid down Jace's body, confirming every one of Tyler's earlier claims. He bit back his I-told-you-so. The middle-aged woman chewed her bottom lip, as if by doing so her thoughts would stay locked behind her teeth. Unfortunately, her eyes said everything she didn't allow her tongue.

"I have to get some supplies from the hotel. If you'd like, you can hang out inside until I return. I'll be back in fifteen minutes. I'm worth the wait."

Tyler bit the inside of his cheek—hard. The urge to laugh was kicking his ass— doubly so since Jace was clueless, and every word the woman spoke was directed Jace's way.

"I'm not sure," Jace said, sounding regretful. "Really, we wanted to check out your services and see if anything caught our eye."

A bright smile lit her face. She waved them inside. "That's fine. There're brochures on the counter. Look over the list and let me know what you need when I get back. If you think you'll still be here, I could bring you a glass of wine from the bar."

Jace didn't look anywhere near as uncomfortable as he should have, considering the woman probably intended to slip a roofie in his drink. "No, thank you. I can't promise we'll still be here, and I don't want to put you out."

"Okay, well, I'll hurry." The woman grabbed a sign and stuck it in the sand in front of the tent's opening, informing everyone she was temporarily closed. "This way, you'll definitely be first when I get back," she said with a wink as she headed out, leaving them alone inside the makeshift hut.

Tyler waited until the woman's shadow

disappeared before speaking up. "She said fifteen minutes. I wonder how accurate that timing is?"

"Why?"

"Because I want to do this," Tyler said, smacking Jace's ass hard enough his palm stung. Jace had it coming, even though Tyler couldn't decide if it was more for not believing him when he said the man was hot, or for letting that woman flirt with him. A low moan filled with longing escaped Jace before Jace bit his bottom lip, stifling the sound.

Tyler's gaze fixated upon him. "Oh my God. You liked that," he accused.

Jace's gaze skittered away. He didn't respond.

Tyler spanked the man again. This time, he was watching, and Jace couldn't hide the desire written in his every line. Lust slammed into Tyler's gut. His dick stood at attention. Tyler's mouth went dry.

He wanted to push Jace, see how far the man would go. After the first time they'd slept together, Tyler had tried taming his nature. Now his kinks were clawing at his skin. He needed to know.

Tyler pulled Jace deeper inside the hut. Once they were somewhat hidden from sight, Tyler dove his hand inside Jace's swim trunks. Jace went from half-hard to stiff in an instant against Tyler's palm. There was no calling his desire back now.

"I want inside you."

Jace's gaze collided with his. "Now?"

Tyler nodded. "I can make you come before the spa woman returns." Without waiting for Jace to agree, Tyler inspected the oils around the massage table. When he found something he could use, he shoved his shorts down and coated his cock in the oily liquid. "Shorts off, Jace. I'm about to fuck you."

Jace glanced around as if looking for an escape. There wasn't one. "What if we get caught?" he hissed.

Tyler stroked himself, taunting Jace with the sight. "Shorts off," he repeated.

With his bottom lip held between his teeth and blushing, Jace shoved his shorts down his hips. Triumph roared through Tyler's veins. He didn't waste any time leaning Jace over the table and pushing his way inside.

"Goddamn," Jace cursed as he took Tyler to the hilt. A woman walked past the opening of the massage stand. They froze. Her back was to them. She paused as if searching for something. Tyler put his hand over Jace's mouth and pivoted his hips, moving slow. He pressed his lips to Jace's ear. "What do you think will happen if she sees?" Jace couldn't answer with his mouth covered. Tyler didn't need a response. The woman moved on, taking away the chance of getting caught. "Too bad," Tyler breathed. "Someone should witness me getting to pound this sexy ass. Damn, the way it grips my dick, pulling me deeper. Fuck. And this," Tyler added, swiping his palm up Jace's erection, wetting his hand with the man's pre-cum. "Goddamn, you're always leaking like you're coming the whole time I'm inside you." He licked his palm, savoring Jace's salt.

Jace whimpered. His ass tightened on Tyler's dick.

"Jesus, Jace." Tyler pumped faster. "Let me see you come on that towel. Please? I need it."

Jace grabbed the towel. He jacked his cock. Tyler tried getting deeper as Jace brought himself pleasure. Jace moaned. Tyler slapped his hand over the man's mouth again. He was too close to get busted now. Jace tongued Tyler's palm.

Tyler's mind went blank. This man would let Tyler do anything to him. He was fucking perfect. His orgasm hit without warning. Thankfully, Jace wasn't far behind him. They rushed through cleaning up before they got thrown out. Even as he swiped away the mess, Tyler couldn't stop staring at Jace. Jace had seriously just let Tyler fuck him in public. The fact they hadn't been seen didn't mean a thing. Tyler's stomach was in knots. All the possibilities crowded his mind.

"What?" Jace asked when Tyler's stare obviously became too much for him.

"Do you really want a massage?"

A slash of white teeth appeared. "I think I'm as relaxed as possible now. Why?"

"I don't want to share you," Tyler admitted, surprising even himself.

*

Jace let Tyler keep him holed up in the room until hunger had him begging for a break. His face burned every time he thought of what they'd done on the beach. Even now, Jace had no clue how Tyler had so easily convinced him to strip inside that hut. Butterflies stirred in his stomach each time he pictured the way Tyler had looked at him before telling him to take off his shorts. After years of feeling unwanted and unattractive, in one heated glance, Tyler had changed Jace's entire mindset. He'd felt powerful—like he'd driven Tyler to the point he couldn't make it back to their room without having Jace. Being with Tyler was liberating in a way Jace couldn't articulate.

They chose a table outside near one of the resort's many pools. There was a bar slash club in a glass-enclosed ballroom within sight. The music inside spilled out into the restaurant, but not so loudly they couldn't hear each other speak. From where they sat, they could see the club's patrons on the dance floor and see the bartender slinging drinks. Jace ordered a daiquiri and Tyler asked for a beer. As they waited for their drinks, Tyler stared at the menu. Jace stared at Tyler.

His beard was getting thick. Damn, Jace loved the way it felt against his bare skin. He had beard burn in so many places, Jace should be blushing. Wasn't happening. Even after hours of playtime, he still wanted to lick the cords of Tyler's neck and beg the man to go back upstairs with him. His stomach growled, reminding him of the food he'd begged for earlier. Tyler's gray eyes lit with humor as he glanced up from the menu and caught Jace staring.

"What are you thinking about?"

"You," Jace answered without an ounce of shame.

Dimples appeared at the corners of Tyler's mouth. "I meant, what are you thinking about getting?"

"Oh." Jace dropped his gaze to his menu. Heat filled his cheeks. "Um. I have no idea. What about you?" he asked, meeting Tyler's stare once more.

Tyler was chewing his bottom lip and watching Jace with hunger in his eyes. Jace could barely breathe. "Let's go back to the room."

A chuckle escaped Jace. "Food. It's time for food," Jace reminded Tyler, hoping he wouldn't give in to temptation. Seriously, they needed to eat if they wanted to keep up this pace.

"They have room service."

Jace wondered why they hadn't thought of this glorious amenity earlier. "That's true." Even Jace was shocked by how levelheaded he sounded, considering how his dick stirred at the realization they could go back to the room and still have dinner.

Tyler cast a quick glance around. "Damn. Where did that waitress—hey. It's Jimmy and Eli."

Jace's head whipped around. Jimmy and Eli were seated two tables over. As if they felt their combined stare, the pair glanced over. Jimmy's bright smile took Jace by surprise. The man had changed so much since meeting Eli. At one time, that bit of knowledge would've bothered Jace. Now he only felt relieved Jimmy hadn't curled up in a bottle and died. Jace glanced Tyler's way. His pride for Jimmy showed in his every line. His own smile grew in response.

"We should invite them to eat with us."

Tyler's gaze shot to Jace's at the offer and lingered. "Are you sure?"

It drove Jace a little crazy Tyler worried over his feelings every second of the day as if his own didn't matter. "Of course. We came here for them. Not to mention, now is your chance to get some quality time with Jimmy."

"I thought you wanted room service."

"For the love of—would you go ask them to join us already?"

Instead of doing as Jace urged, Tyler waved at them and pointed at the empty seats at their table. Eli and Jimmy exchanged words before coming to their feet.

A snort left Jace. "Or you could wave them over."

Tyler winked. "You've had me hard since agreeing to go back upstairs. No way was I walking up to Jimmy with my hard dick all in his face."

A bark of laughter escaped Jace. He slapped his hand over his mouth, trying to hold back the sound.

"I'm surprised to see you here this

early," Eli said, pulling their focus his way.

Tyler sounded happy when he responded. His tone had Jace's smile growing by the second. "We decided to come a few days early and get in a much-needed vacation."

The pair moved their chairs closer before sitting. Jimmy looked at Jace. "I know it's been decades since Tyler's had any time off. How long has it been for you?"

Jace shrugged. "I don't know if it counts as a vacation, but I went to New York a few months ago with Adam to help him find a place to live."

"Adam is living in New York?"

"Who's Adam?" Eli asked at the same time.

Jimmy answered, saving Jace from having to explain. "He's Jace's nephew. Jace has raised him since his parents passed several years ago."

Eli nodded.

Jace answered Jimmy's earlier question. "He moved to New York to take an internship, doing makeup for stars and models."

"That's amazing," Eli said. His sweet smile gave Jace the impression he meant it.

Tyler linked his fingers through Jace's under the table. Jace's spine relaxed against the chair at the contact. "Yeah, well, he's young. He should get at least one chance to follow his dreams. I'm glad he was brave enough to take the leap." As Jace said the words, he realized Adam and Eli were probably very close to being the same age. It was almost funny. At one time, he'd seen Eli as young too, but now he'd gotten to know the man. Now Eli seemed closer to the rest of them in age. Life had aged him well beyond his years.

The waitress showed up with two

waters with lemon and saved Jace from saying as much aloud. "I thought I'd lost you two for a minute there," she said, setting the waters in front of them.

"We spotted family and decided to join them," Jimmy said, answering for them. Tyler's grip tightened on Jace's hand at the claim.

"It's a small world," she said, sounding as if she was merely holding up her end. "Is everyone ready to order?" As she went around the table, taking everyone's order, Jace stared at Tyler's profile. Jimmy had called the man family again. Tyler's reaction made Jace want to take back everything he'd said outside the gym that day. At the time, he'd been angry and hurt. He hadn't considered how his words cut. Now he realized how much Jimmy meant to Tyler. He was the same with Jimmy as Jace was with Adam. Jace wanted them to have a real shot at being family.

Jace waited until their server left them alone before speaking up. "So, Jimmy, you must have some awesome stories about Tyler."

Jimmy brought Eli's hand to his mouth and pressed his lips to the back of it before responding. "Not me. I'm not the one with the stories. Tyler is the one who used to come home and tell me about all the craziness he dealt with that day."

"Really?" Jace asked. Even he could hear the disbelief in his voice. Tyler never talked about work.

A low chuckle rumbled from Tyler. "I was a patrol officer back then. Things were different. I could see the humor in the bullshit. Now there's nothing about my job I want to talk about."

"I think I want to hear some of these stories," Eli said, keeping the conversation rolling.

Every time Tyler glanced Eli's way, his

expression underwent a subtle change. He became softer, as if adjusting to Eli's needs. This man, he was so fucking amazing. Jace's heart swelled with pride.

"I pulled over the governor for speeding once."

"Gave him a ticket too," Jimmy added.

Tyler shook with laughter. Yet he still traced a pattern on Jace's hand without stopping. "In my defense, I didn't like him."

Jimmy took a sip of water. "Is that still a black mark on your record?"

"It was worth it," Tyler said with a shrug.

Jace couldn't concentrate. Tyler's hair fell in just the right way. Good humor shone brightly in the man's eyes. He was perfect. "You're amazing." Tyler's gaze moved to Jace. His mouth lifted in one corner, making him look cocky. Jace's mouth watered in response. God help

Jace. He might kill anyone if they tried taking this man from him.

*

Tyler could barely concentrate with Jace watching him the way he was. There was so much heat coming from Jace's stare, Tyler wondered if anything he said made sense. He was on top of the world and didn't have enough words to express his jubilation. Tyler wondered if his body would withstand the torment of this dinner. Their bed called his name. He somehow made it through the meal by telling tale after tale of his time on the force. Every time he thought the topic had gone stale, Jimmy remembered another one.

"Tell the story of the orange juice ass whoopin'. I still crack up when I think about it," Jimmy said, pulling Tyler's focus away from eating Jace alive with his gaze.

Tyler snorted at Jimmy's request. "Ha.

I'd forgotten all about that." Jace stared at him expectantly. There was no way he was passing up on holding Jace's attention. "Okay, so when I first started as a patrol officer, I got a call about an attempted robbery in the parking lot of an apartment complex. When I showed up, there was this tiny blonde woman sitting calmly on the curb with a gallon of orange juice by her feet. The EMTs were treating this behemoth of a woman. She was covered in tattoos and looked mean as hell, but she was also bleeding from several cuts on her face, arms, and head. Anyhow, as I approached the little blonde, she smiled up at me. She had such a sweet smile. When she spoke, her voice was soft and with deference to my position. So, I asked her what happened."

Having already heard the story, Jimmy chuckled. Tyler bit back a laugh and continued. "She said she'd pulled into her usual parking space and popped the trunk of her car to get out her groceries. When she circled the car, the other woman had approached her, saying, 'You shouldn't leave your trunk standing open while you carry your groceries in. Someone might steal your shit.' The blonde said the way the other woman spoke immediately had her hackles up. She told the tattoo lady, 'One, I'm still standing here, so no one's stealing from me. B, mind your business.' At the lecture, the tattooed woman reached around her and snagged a gallon of orange juice and calmly walked away. She said, 'I thought, oh, this bitch thinks I won't fight her. Long story short, I got my juice back,' she said toeing the gallon at her feet." Tyler swiped his eyes. "I couldn't believe what I was hearing. This other woman was four times the size of this tiny blonde. Before I could temper my reaction, I said, 'What the hell were you thinking?

She could've killed you. What if she'd had a gun? Or a knife? Or hell, she could've beaten your head into the pavement. All for a gallon of juice.' The woman shrugged and said, 'I was thinking I'd stood in line behind some hooch super-couponing for twenty minutes to get that orange juice.' She looked at me and her face hardened. I almost took a step back because I could see the crazy in her eyes. She said, 'Bet she don't steal again.'"

Jace's laughter made Tyler wish he could keep him that way forever.

"I'm guessing you have thousands of these stories."

Tyler nodded. "But most involve pulling over people with objects shoved up their ass. Drugs, live ammunition, sex toys while just out for a drive. Seriously, we're living in a generation of people with crazy shit up their asses."

Tyler had to force himself to stop

staring at the way Jace's eyes shone with happiness. He focused on Eli and Jimmy. At some point, he'd lost them. They were sitting with their heads together, quietly talking. Pride rose in Tyler's chest and choked him. All this. This was what he'd dreamed of for Jimmy—a normal life. Happiness. Jimmy deserved all of it. He'd paid for it in blood. Tyler blinked. His eyes burned. He wished there was some way he could express how he felt, but Jimmy would never accept it. This was as close as they'd ever be. It had to be enough.

Jimmy's head jerked up, as if he heard something in the distance. He smiled at Eli. "They're playing the first song we ever danced to. Let's go." He stood and grabbed Eli's hand, all but dragging Eli from his seat. Eli's laughter let Tyler know he wasn't bothered. As the door to the bar opened, music spilled out. Tyler could see the pair through the glass. He watched as

Jimmy pulled Eli into his arms on the dance floor.

"You're so fucking proud you can't stand it," Jace said, capturing Tyler's attention.

Tyler flashed Jace a sad smile. "When I took Jimmy in, he was like an injured wolf. He snapped and snarled. I knew he'd either heal or rip my throat out while I slept."

"Why'd you do it?" Jace asked, taking Tyler by surprise. "I mean, no one would've batted an eye had you taken him to a foster-care home and left him to his fate. That's what any one of your co-workers would've done."

Tyler's lips twisted into a sad smile. He reached over and took Jace's hand before bringing it to his lips. "You don't want to hear this."

Jace looked thoughtful. "Yeah, I think

I do. It's part of you, and I'm coming to realize I want all of you."

Whoa. That was more than Tyler had been expecting. If that was what Jace wanted, then he should see how ugly Tyler's life was, because it wouldn't get better in the future. The world got a little nastier every day. "Tell me to stop if I'm telling you more than you can handle, okay?"

Jace nodded.

Tyler took a deep breath. "That guy who held Jimmy for six years, his name was Matthew Stephens. He raped and murdered more than twenty kids." Saying those words out loud still felt like razorblades in Tyler's throat. To this day, he didn't understand how anyone ever let their kids out of their sight. "He molested countless others. I imagine we'll never know a true number. See, there used to be this drug dealer who would sell you anything for the right price. If a person wanted to sell the pleasure of their child's company for their next hit, this guy knew just the buyer—Matthew. All of those kids got off lucky, even the ones who died, because they weren't Jimmy. Something about Jimmy held Matthew enthralled." Tyler swallowed. He hoped somewhere in Hell, Matthew was getting the devil's personal attention. "The first time I saw Jimmy, he was covered in blood from slitting Matthew's throat. He sat there calmly as if nothing had happened. It was another day. But it only took one look in his eyes to see he was dead on the inside. Despite all of that, I wanted to hug him. Jimmy had done something I'd wanted to do for years; he'd killed the man who raped and murdered my little brother."

Tyler fell silent. There were a thousand

more thoughts he could tell Jace—like how Jimmy wouldn't have gotten the treatment he needed in foster care. But, in the end, it boiled down to one thing—Jimmy was the executioner who'd brought Tyler justice. Jace hadn't run away, but Tyler still couldn't bring himself to look Jace's way. Tyler cleared his throat. "He's the same age as my brother, you know? They even share the same birthday. It's as if it was fated."

"What was your brother's name?" Jace asked, startling Tyler out of his dark thoughts.

"Caleb," Tyler said, still not looking Jace's way. "Don't tell, okay?" Tyler said, finally meeting Jace's stare. Tyler snorted. "I'm sorry. You're not that kind of person. I know you won't say anything."

"I'm surprised that tidbit didn't turn up in that book written on Jimmy's life."

Tyler growled before he could call it back. "That fucking book." Some asshat had made a fortune exploiting Jimmy's life. "I've tried a hundred times to talk Jimmy into suing that fucker. He wants to leave it all behind him and suing will drag everything up again. I know he's right, but fuck. It drives me insane knowing that bastard is making a single dime off Jimmy's pain."

"Where's he live? Let's slash his tires."

A roar of laughter hit Tyler unexpectedly at Jace's suggestion. Tyler snorted before he could call it back. "You're a little evil under all that sexy. I love it." To his surprise, Jace's smile fell at his words. Tyler wanted Jace's happiness back. He leaned closer to Jace and held his stare while whispering his confession. "In fact, that's not all I've come to love about you. Actually, I'm in love with everything about you, except your singing. That's something only your momma could love."

Jace punched Tyler in the arm. "Shut up. It's not nice to tease people."

Tyler caught Jace's fist and held it. He brushed his thumb over Jace's knuckles. "I'm just playing. I love your singing too. Actually, I'm just in love with you."

Jace's jaw dropped before his teeth audibly snapped together.

Tyler scoffed. "Come on now. It can't be that big of a surprise. I spend every free moment with you and can't get enough of you."

"Lusting someone isn't the same as loving them," Jace argued, even though there wasn't any real heat behind his words.

"Seriously, Jace. Do you honestly think this is only lust?"

For a minute, all Jace did was stare at Tyler and blink. "Not for me, no."

It was Tyler's turn to blink. "I'm equal parts ecstatic and insulted and can't decide why."

Jace's mouth lifted in one corner, showing off just one dimple. "Probably because we just failed epically in saying our first I love yous."

"Fuck that," Tyler said from the bottom of his soul. "No way am I looking back on this moment as a failure. Come here," he said, snagging the front of Jace's shirt and dragging him forward. Once they were nose to nose, Tyler held Jace's stare. "Length of time together doesn't mean shit. My heart chose you. I love you."

Jace pressed his lips together, visibly

fighting back a smile. Once he appeared to have it under control, he cleared his throat. "I love you too." As soon as the confession left him, a smile exploded across Jace's face. "Holy shit. I just said that and I'm not even scared."

"You don't ever have to be, babe. I've got you now."

"Yeah, you do," Jace agreed. He cast a quick glance around as if searching for something. "I'm going to run to the restroom, okay? I'll be right back."

Tyler nodded. "All right, babe. I'll be here." Tyler took a sip of his drink and leaned back in his chair. The night air brushed over his skin. He was happy—like he hadn't been in a really long while. Maybe he could talk Jace into staying a few days longer? Jace's phone rang, startling him. Tyler hadn't even seen it sitting there. After sitting forward, he checked out the face. It was Paige. Tyler answered.

"Hello?"

"Who the hell is this?"

Tyler blew out a sigh. Paige was one of the most abrasive people he'd ever met and that was saying a lot, being as how he'd raised Jimmy. "It's Tyler."

"What the fuck are you doing answering Jace's phone? Don't you trust him?"

While rubbing the spot between his eyes that ached at the sound of her voice, Tyler snorted. "He's in the restroom and we're at dinner. I didn't want his phone disturbing the people who are seated around us trying to enjoy their meal."

"Well, hang up. I didn't call to talk to you."

"Wow," Tyler breathed before he could call it back. "I'll let him know you called." Without giving her time to respond, Tyler hung up on her.

Jace reappeared. "Who was that?"

Tyler tried damn hard to keep the hatred from his voice as he answered. "Paige."

"Oh," Jace said, not sounding any more happy than Tyler. That piqued Tyler's curiosity, but he wouldn't ask. Jace turned his phone off without returning her call.

"You can call her back. I don't mind." Jace would never know how it pained Tyler to say those words. He harbored a secret hatred of Paige, but she was Jace's best friend, so he stamped it down.

Jace shook his head. "I mind. This is our time. She knows that. I only had my phone on in case Adam needed me. Anything Paige has to say would be drama, and I'm on vacation."

He wanted to ask why Jace wanted to be friends with someone so exhausting, but he kept the question to himself. They'd known each other a long time. Tyler knew from experience sometimes those friendships were hard to shake, especially in the day and age of social media. People were connected in a million ways. Not to mention, she knew where Jace lived, and she struck Tyler as crazy.

A glass of white wine appeared at Jace's elbow, pulling Tyler from his musings. "The glass of wine I promised you earlier," Spa Lady said, coming out of nowhere.

"Wow. Thank you," Jace said, sounding every bit as grateful as his words suggested. Tyler couldn't believe the man was so blind. "That's so nice of you."

She winked. "I always keep my promises." She stuck out her hand. "I'm Jana, by the way. It occurs to me I didn't introduce myself earlier."

Jace accepted her handshake. "Jace."

"What an awesome name," Jana said. She pushed a curl behind her ear and rocked back on her heels before cramming her hands in the front pockets of her jeans. The move somehow managed to pull her shirt down an inch, revealing a generous amount of cleavage. "If you get lonely, I'm at the bar."

A line appeared between Jace's eyes, making Tyler wonder if Jace intended to point out he wasn't alone. Instead, he flashed his sweetest smile. "Thank you. I'll keep that in mind."

With another smoldering inspection of Jace's body, she gave Jace a short nod. "Hopefully, I'll see you soon," Jana said before heading for the same door Jimmy and Eli had disappeared through.

The instant they were alone, Jace cast a desperate look around. "Should I pour it out? Is she looking?"

A roar of laughter escaped Tyler as he realized Jace wasn't as clueless as he'd pretended to be. Tyler snuck a peek at the bar. She was looking. "Oh, yeah," Tyler said, hating to confirm Jace's fear. "Her gaze is locked on you like a lion stalking prey."

"Oh my God." His horrified whisper had Tyler fighting back his smile. "I don't want to hurt her feelings. She obviously doesn't realize we're together." His shoulders fell. Defeat was written in his every line. Tyler got it. Jace was nice, and he didn't like making anyone feel unwanted, even if they were.

"It's fine, baby. I got this." Tyler rearranged his chair and reached for his beer. As he did, he accidentally on purpose knocked over the glass of wine. Jace's shooting to his feet appeared genuine, because it was.

There weren't any napkins on the table besides the cocktail napkins under their drinks. Their waitress rushed over, helping to clean away the mess. Tyler apologized several times, just in case the waitress knew the spa lady.

"Can you do me a favor?" he asked the waitress, pulling her attention his way. He pointed toward where Jana sat. "Do you see that woman sitting there?"

After casting a quick glance Jana's way, she nodded. "Yep. She works at the resort's spa," she said, proving Tyler's suspicions.

"Will you take her a glass of champagne and offer her my apologies for spilling her wine?" He handed her two twenties to sweeten the deal.

201

As the money exchanged hands, the waitress' smile grew. "Of course."

While he had Jace on his feet, Tyler set his hand on the small of Jace's back, urging the man toward the closest elevator. "Time for dessert, baby."

Jace glanced over his shoulder. "What about Jimmy and Eli?"

Tyler's steps didn't slow. "Sweetheart, they were headed back to their room halfway through their first dance."

"Oh." Jace chuckled. The sound caressed Tyler's ears. "I never saw them leave."

The elevator door slid open. Finding it empty, Tyler crowded Jace inside. He kept moving until Jace's back hit the wall and the door closed them inside.

"You have to hit the button for our floor or we'll never get there," Jace reminded him with laughter lacing each word.

Tyler growled over having to give up touching his man. He quickly hit the seven and went back to holding Jace. His eyes fell closed as their bodies collided. They fit perfectly. Every time Tyler thought about him, thinking—for even a moment—he could give this man up, he was ashamed of his weakness. Only a fool would sneak from this man's bed. Jace should've made him suffer—grovel. Instead, he'd quietly forgiven Tyler. Damn, Jace hadn't even mentioned it again. Tyler wasn't worthy of that type of forgiveness. He buried his face in the crook of Jace's neck and inhaled.

"I love you."

At Tyler's confession, Jace shoved both hands underneath Tyler's T-shirt and held on. "I love you too." Jace sounded breathless. A dark hunger rose in Tyler. No one had said those words to him in years. He wanted to hear them again, in every tone. Tyler craved knowing how they sounded, tearing from Jace's lips on the verge of orgasm. He even needed to know how they sounded when Jace was enraged and exasperated with Tyler. In his heart, Tyler already knew he'd never tire of hearing those three words on Jace's tongue.

By the time the elevator door opened again, setting them free, Tyler was on the verge of promising Jace anything he wanted as long as he never stole those words from him. He couldn't go back to never hearing them. The loss would kill him. Jace's laughter followed him down the hallway as Tyler raced to the room, dragging Jace along with him. He needed to get this man alone and give Jace a reason to keep him. Right now, they didn't feel square. Surely Tyler didn't give him as much as Jace did for Tyler.

The instant their hotel door closed them away from the world, Tyler turned to

Jace and held his gaze. "Tell me what you want."

Jace's nose curled, the way it always did while he tried puzzling through Tyler's words. "You'll have to be more specific. I mean, I have you, and that's all I want. Unless you're talking about something else—like, what I want out of life or what I want to eat tomorrow." Jace laughed. It was a nervous sound. "See? I need more to go on."

"Yes," Tyler said, doing his part to further muddy the waters.

Jace twisted his fingers and glanced around the room as if that would help him figure out Tyler. "Um... what?"

Despite the odd change his mood had undergone, a smile spread across Tyler's face. "Exactly. What, Jace? What do you want out of life? I'm dying to know what you want to eat tomorrow and the day after that. Tell me in what way you'll rock

205

my world next. What do you want from me, from us?"

Jace stared at him in silence for so long Tyler wondered if the man was plotting his escape. His expression gave nothing away. He eyed Jace while holding his own council until Tyler thought he'd scream. When Jace finally spoke, he did what he always did. Jace rocked him to his soul. "Don't break me. That's what I want. I need for you to never tear down this beautiful thing we're building. Don't make me wonder if it was all lies or I'm a fool. The thing is—I don't know what it'll take for you give to me what I want, because I've never had it."

Tyler closed the distance between them. "Don't worry. I know how to give you what you need," he said as he buried his fingers in Jace's hair. With a tug, he pulled the man closer and covered Jace's mouth. As always, when their lips met, the world disappeared and fire consumed him. Tyler didn't know if he'd survive the weekend.

*

With their bare feet planted in the sand and waves lapping at their ankles, Tyler and Jace stood at Jimmy and Eli's back, witnessing them exchange their vows. A lump moved into Tyler's throat. He feared it was permanent. Never in his wildest dreams had he expected to see this day. To his shame, Tyler had secretly believed Jimmy would kill himself eventually. The man had been trying to do it with alcohol for years, but Tyler expected he'd eat a bullet or drive his truck off a cliff. It would've killed Tyler. But honestly, Tyler didn't know what had kept Jimmy fighting before Eli.

Now there was Eli, and he stood so proud and strong at Jimmy's side. The urge to pull Eli into a bear hug was overwhelming. Until the day he died, Eli would have Tyler's love and respect. Eli and Jimmy kissed. Without thought, Tyler tugged Jace closer. There was no one else Tyler would rather have at his side. He hadn't been lying when he'd told Jace he loved him. This was real. He would fight to keep it.

Jace's grip tightened on his hand.

Tyler glanced over.

Jace mouthed, "Are you okay?"

With a nod, Tyler mouthed, "I love you," because he couldn't say it enough.

Jace winked.

He never wanted to leave this place. Without thought, he towed Jace into his arms and covered the man's mouth in a searching kiss. The tongues met and retreated. Heat exploded through Tyler's body. He wanted to consume Jace. The desire to crawl inside the man's head, set up shop, and take over his life was a real thing.

Someone cleared their throat. A blush climbed up his cheeks as he realized what he'd done. The older man who officiated the wedding was watching them. The man's eyes danced with humor.

"Am I marrying you today too?"

Chapter 7

December

Jace had learned two things in the past few months. One, he should never have dinner waiting, because it was always cold before Tyler got home. Two, he shouldn't bother waiting up. Since tomorrow was Christmas Eve, Jace was staring down the barrel of two glorious weeks off. That was the awesome thing about working private practice. His boss always closed up shop this time of year to be with her kids for the holidays. That meant Jace had nowhere to be. He was free to wait up for Tyler as long as he liked.

It had been an odd day. One that left Jace in a strange mood. That was why, after firing up the fireplace and pulling the cork on a bottle of wine, he plopped his ass on the couch and hadn't moved. Jace glanced over at his glass. Oops. Make that two bottles. He hadn't bothered with the lights or TV. The way the orange flames cast a dancing glow on the walls of the silent room was entertainment enough.

He'd surpassed a light buzz over an hour ago. Now he was deep in wishing Tyler was home so he could do bad things to him territory. As if the universe felt his need and wanted him to get fucked, Tyler came through the back door. From his vantage point, he could see Tyler unstrapping his gun and leaving it on the counter. When he turned, Jace's heart fell. A dark scowl marred Tyler's features. It had been one of those days. A day where Tyler had seen shit he wouldn't talk about and Jace didn't want to hear about. Luckily, he knew how to fix him.

Tyler leaned his shoulder into the living room's doorframe and crossed his arms over his chest. As he eyed the empty wine bottles and took in the entire scene, Jace eyed the way the muscles moved in Tyler's forearms. Damn. He wanted this man.

"Why are you sitting in the dark?"

Jace patted the spot between his knees, beckoning Tyler closer. "Just enjoying the silence. Come here. You look like you need some TLC."

A small smile touched Tyler's lips. He crossed the room. His lips lightly brushed Jace's before he dropped down to the floor between Jace's knees and leaned his head back into Jace's lap. This had become their thing. This was all Jace knew how to do to ease Tyler's burden. His fingers found Tyler's soft locks. In the same pattern as always, Jace dragged his fingers through Tyler's hair while massaging the man's scalp. Tyler's eyes fell closed and his face relaxed. Jace loved these moments. Not only was he free to enjoy staring at Tyler unimpeded, he also brought comfort to Tyler's life.

"Tell me what I can do." Jace already knew Tyler's response. It was always the same.

"You're doing it."

Jace's cell phone chirped, alerting him of an incoming text. He swallowed down his irritation over the interruption and checked his phone. In his heart, he already knew what he'd see, but he couldn't ignore it in case it was Adam.

Paige: *This is message number 5. You can stop ignoring me now.*

Jace: *I'm not ignoring you. Tyler just got home.*

Paige: *Just now? No one works that many hours all the time. You need to start checking his phone. That's some shady shit.*

Jace drew a deep breath through his nose before deciding he wouldn't respond.

He turned his phone off and went back to massaging Tyler's scalp.

Tyler released a happy sounding sigh. "Paige or Adam?"

"Paige," Jace said, trying to keep any emotion from showing in his voice.

Tyler never opened his eyes. "Did you ever find out if Adam is coming home for Christmas?"

"Yeah. He won't get to stay long, but he's flying in on Christmas Day and back to New York the next."

"That boss of his is no joke."

"Mmm," Jace said noncommittally. Jace had his own thoughts about why Adam was reluctant to leave New York for long, but he had nothing to go on but his gut.

"You think he's met someone," Tyler said, as if pulling the thoughts from Jace's head.

"That's my guess." Jace changed

directions and rubbed Tyler's temples. Damn, he loved the way Tyler felt beneath his fingertips.

A line appeared between Tyler's closed eyes. "I hope whoever it is knows I own a gun."

A low chuckle rumbled from Jace. "It's sexy when you get all protective."

Tyler's face smoothed and his lips curled into a gorgeous smile. Jace didn't miss a single nuance. He barely blinked as he eyed every changing detail of Tyler's expression. "I take care of my own."

Without thought, Jace bent and brushed his lips over Tyler's. He didn't try to deepen their kiss. The angle was too awkward, but he couldn't resist those sexy lips a moment longer.

"Mmm," Tyler growled, reminding Jace of earlier lust. "How was your day, by the way?"

Jace ran both hands through Tyler's

hair, leaving it standing on end. He smiled at the mess he made. Jace didn't want to talk about his day but couldn't avoid it forever.

"Can I talk to you about something?"

"Please," Tyler said immediately. "It'll give me something to think about besides this awful day."

Jace kept brushing his fingers through Tyler's hair, and Tyler didn't open his eyes. Those two details comforted him, allowing him to speak freely. "My boss offered me a job at the Nashville location today. More money. Less hours. That location is only open three days a week, and it's this side of Nashville, so the drive wouldn't be horrendous."

Tyler didn't respond right away, but Jace knew he was the type of person who weighed every word before speaking, especially when it was important. "You sound like you want to accept."

"I do."

Dimples appeared at the corners of Tyler's mouth, making Jace's stomach cramp with need. "But?"

Jace bit the bullet and let the words fly. "I'm not sure Nashville is far enough away for what I really need."

Tyler's eyes opened. He rolled to his knees and wrapped his arms around Jace's hips. His gaze searched Jace's face, as if he could look hard enough and uncover all Jace's secrets. "Question."

"Yeah," Jace said, his voice coming out small.

"Are you trying to get away from Paige?"

Jace's shoulders fell. He felt disloyal. "Yes." He took a deep breath. Once it was out there, Jace couldn't stop. "I feel like a complete douche for wanting to get away from her. She's been my best friend for nine years, but..." A sound of total disgust escaped Jace. He couldn't call it back.

"She's crazy and makes your life miserable."

"Yes." The cry felt like vindication leaving his lips. Jace wasn't alone. He wasn't the only one who saw it. "Maybe it's my fault. I'm the one who's changed."

"For the better," Tyler said, adding his thoughts.

Jace didn't slow. "But she's so possessive and hateful. Do you know, she makes all these small comments about you and acts like she's just making conversation, but really she's undermining everything we have, and I hate it. Every morning, I drive to work, wondering how many more days I have to drive to work, because I can't listen to another spiteful word. I know she'll insinuate at least once you're cheating on me, and that I'm failing her as a friend." Jace held Tyler's stare. He lowered his voice to a whisper because he was tired. "I'm not sure I can do it anymore."

Tyler's gaze seemed to turn inward. Jace couldn't look away from the way Tyler chewed his bottom lip as he mulled over whatever was inside his head. Finally, Tyler focused on Jace once more. "I have a confession too. I'm burned out."

Jace didn't know what to say. He'd wondered for a while now how Tyler kept going all the time.

"Tell me how to help," Jace said, needing to do something.

Tyler smiled. "Let's run away together."

A bark of laughter escaped Jace. It died when Tyler's expression never changed. "You're serious."

Even though it hadn't been a question, Tyler nodded. "Jimmy is married now, so he doesn't need me here, making sure he doesn't do something to get himself killed.

Adam is in New York. We both raised other people's kids, starting at a young age. I think we should just go and be us for a while."

Jace took the suggestion seriously. It wasn't as if they couldn't afford it. Tyler worked so much and he never spent any money. Jace's dad had passed five years ago, leaving him everything. There was no reason they couldn't take some time and just go.

A slow smile pulled at the corners of Jace's mouth. "Dr. Swanson already has someone lined up to take over my position in case I wanted the Nashville job."

"See? It's fate," Tyler said, sounding hopeful.

"And I have always wanted to go to Australia."

Tyler nodded. "They have beaches there. I'm happy to plant my ass in the sand anywhere in the world."

Jace couldn't believe he was considering this. "We really could just pick up and go, couldn't we?"

Tyler's arms tightened on Jace's waist. His smile grew as he nodded. It was the first time in a while Jace had seen the man this happy. That had him decided without further enticement, but Tyler kept talking. "If you'd like, and you're serious, we can go tomorrow, before the stores close for the holidays, and change your number. We could be out of here before the new year."

Jace thought of one more thing before he agreed. "Do you really think you can give up having 'Detective' in front of your name?"

"Absolutely. After all, you gave up your last name for me."

Butterflies stirred in Jace's stomach. "Then let's do it."

Tyler blinked as if he hadn't honestly

believed Jace would accept. His surprise slowly slipped from his features, replaced with a level of excitement Jace hadn't seen since Miami. His gaze turned heated as it slid down Jace's body. "I really have you now. All to myself. Damn. What should I do first?"

An involuntary moan escaped Jace at the sex dripping from Tyler's words.

Tyler's gaze sharpened. He licked his lips. "How horny are you after those two bottles of wine?"

"Oh God," Jace whimpered. "Want you *so* bad."

"How can I make it better?"

Jace took the question seriously before answering, "I'm really hoping you'll let me play with your dick."

Tyler's face flushed. His lips parted on a pant. Jace's dick leaked. "Let's go," Tyler said, pulling Jace to his feet.

Despite his lust, Jace tried slowing

Tyler's progress to the bedroom. "Wait. You need to eat first."

"You're all the feast I need," Tyler said, dragging Jace behind him.

That was a hard argument to counter, so Jace let Tyler have his way.

*

Tyler couldn't get Jace to the bedroom fast enough. He knew from experience how Jace's inhibitions went out the window after a few drinks. Sober, the man would do anything. Drunk, he'd do things that made even Tyler blush. They barely made it to the bedroom before Jace tore at the button of Tyler's jeans. Tyler helped. He wanted skin-on-skin every bit as badly as Jace. While Jace peeled off his clothes, Tyler worked on his own. Before he could reach for Jace, once they were both nude, Jace dropped to his knees and took Tyler to the back of his throat. Tyler's knees tried giving out. Jace was relentless.

Everything about the man's blowjob was perfection.

Jace kept a steady pace and the right amount of pressure while taking all of him. He didn't neglect any of Tyler's hot spots. Jace massaged his balls and fingered Tyler's asshole. All Tyler could do was fuck the man's willing mouth and pray he could hang on, because he didn't want to come this way. He loved being inside Jace when his orgasms hit. The way Jace's ass would squeeze and tug, milking every drop of cum from Tyler's body. Fuck. He loved that shit. Too late, Tyler realized he should've been trying to think of other things if he hoped to last. Jace's throat tightened around Tyler's cock. Tyler's vision narrowed to a pinpoint as a spiral of ecstasy overtook him. He had to lock his knees as the first wave hit, filling Jace's mouth with jet after jet of hot cum. Jace lapped away at that shit as if it was his reward for the day. Tyler couldn't stop staring down at the bliss written in Jace's features. Damn. There was no one else better than him. He was everything to Tyler.

Still, this wasn't how Tyler had wanted things to play out. "Just give me like two minutes, baby," Tyler swore while running his hands through Jace's hair. "I'll be ready to fuck you like you deserve."

Jace's eyes moved upward, meeting Tyler's gaze. He smiled around Tyler's cock but didn't stop sucking. Tyler took a deep breath. He had a feeling he'd need strength. Before even he saw it coming, another wave of pleasure rolled over him, pulling more jets of semen from him. His hand shot out, finding the closest piece of furniture for support. Never in his life had that happened to him. Over the years, he'd heard men brag about multiple orgasms, but honestly, he'd always thought it was bullshit. Goddamn. He couldn't catch his breath. His legs were fucking jelly and Jace was still fucking his ass with his fingers while licking away all evidence of Tyler's orgasm. This man. Goddamn. He was a sickness. Tyler wanted to make him scream.

Before Jace could do anything more to blow his mind, Tyler urged him onto his feet. He found the man's mouth as he maneuvered him onto the bed. Getting inside Jace would have to wait for another night. Right now, he wanted to bring his man as much pleasure as possible. Jace needed to get on this level with him. His lips found Jace's throat. He loved the way the cords in Jace's neck felt against his lips. Tyler didn't linger for long. He didn't want to miss all the sexy, hard muscles Jace worked his ass off to keep. Damn, this man was delicious. Tyler had been to every fight the man entered since the first one Jace let him attend. It was easily the hottest shit Tyler had ever seen. Every single time, they came home and Tyler attacked the man, needing to taste the way his muscles flexed as Jace used his strength against others.

Jace was such a conundrum. He was the sweetest person Tyler had ever met, but he fought like he was the meanest. There were no words to describe how hard that made Tyler's dick. He tongued every muscle between Jace's mouth and his dick. Once he reached the man's cock, Tyler barely let his cheek brush Jace's erection as Tyler kissed the man's oblique. He knew the way his beard tickled would make Jace insane. Judging by how Jace writhed beneath him, Tyler had been right. His smile felt evil as he moved to Jace's navel. Tyler licked a wet circle around it, once again, allowing his beard to tickle Jace's crown. Jace yanked on his hair, trying to force Tyler's mouth to his dick. Tyler chuckled against Jace's skin. It sounded wicked even to his ears. Jace huffed and Tyler took mercy.

In one quick motion, Tyler swallowed Jace's cock. Without an ounce of regret, he also shoved two fingers inside Jace. He knew it probably stung, but Jace had already shown his hand a few times in the past. He liked it when Tyler hurt him. Of course, Tyler would never do any real damage to Jace. Just the thought of anything or anyone marring this beautiful man's skin made Tyler want to kill someone. Saliva ran down Jace's dick, giving Tyler some moisture to ease his entry into Jace's ass. He added a third finger to the mix. He'd wanted to go slow and torture the man beneath him. Instead, Tyler couldn't stop fucking Jace with his fingers, wishing it was his dick. His cock obviously agreed. Against all laws of nature, since it should be dead, his erection leaked onto the sheets, begging to be inside Jace. He wouldn't give in yet. He needed Jace's orgasm. Tyler sucked hard, determined to have it. Jace cried out. Hot cum filled Tyler's mouth. He swallowed even as he crawled higher up the bed.

Jace accepted Tyler's bruising kiss, even with his tongue still covered in Jace's semen. He probed Jace's asshole, seeking entry. The tight ring of muscles gave way, and Jace's body took over, pulling Tyler deeper inside. Tyler expected, since he'd come twice already, he'd last a long time, but no. Jace's orgasm was a hard one. His body convulsed with it, tightening down on Tyler's dick, threatening to hobble him even as it massaged another powerful orgasm from Tyler.

Tyler tore his mouth from Jace's. He couldn't catch his breath. "Holy fuck. Goddamn, Jace. You're fucking killing me.

You're so tight and hot. Fuck."

Jace had no mercy. He pulled Tyler's head down and sucked his bottom lip. Tyler felt sure his lip would sport a hickey tomorrow that would be fun explaining to everyone at Christmas. He didn't fucking care. Every nerve in his body was lit and dancing with joy. Tyler rode out the final waves before rolling to his side so he wouldn't squash Jace. His gaze never left Jace. The man was a sensual feast for Tyler's eyes. He didn't want to give him up.

"Goddamn," Jace breathed, making Tyler want to pat himself on the back. "I fucking love you."

A smile exploded across Tyler's face at Jace's claim. He didn't know what he'd done to deserve this man, but he wouldn't stop trying to earn him. "I love you too, baby."

"Holy shit. My head is spinning." Jace's eyes never opened as he made the claim.

"That's probably the alcohol," Tyler said, making Jace chuckle. Tyler fucking loved that sound. Jace's chest moved in time with every labored breath. Tyler would know. He couldn't stop watching him. The movement finally slowed, falling into a steady pattern. It was hilarious how fast Jace went to sleep. Tyler was too pumped to join him. Watching Jace unimpeded was too much fun. Damn. He was in love with this man. Tyler couldn't stop staring at Jace's perfect features. His long lashes moved as if Jace was caught in a dream. The flush still tinting Jace's cheeks had Tyler wanting to kiss the man awake. Jace would let him, but Tyler would feel like shit for not letting him rest. His giddiness level hit a new high with every passing second. They would soon be spending every waking second together. Tyler already knew he'd never get sick of being with Jace. They were one of those rare cases of love at first sight—a meeting of the souls. He'd found his other half. Now he just wanted to bask in it. He never would've dreamed Jace would be willing to leave his job for this.

Tyler's happiness dimmed a bit. Fucking Paige. He'd known she was an unhappy bitch, but he'd had no idea she'd been insinuating Tyler was a cheat. As if anyone else could please him after Jace. He couldn't think of a punishment evil enough for anyone who tried harming Jace.

The sound of glass breaking brought Tyler's head up. He rolled to his side, trying not to wake Jace as he went for his gun. It wasn't there. Son of a bitch. He'd left it on the kitchen counter. Jace kept a bat under his bed. It wouldn't do him much good if their intruder already had Tyler's gun. No way would Tyler let any harm come to Jace.

After slipping from the bed, Tyler pulled on his boxers, snagged the bat, and sneaked from the room. Whoever was inside wasn't trying to be quiet. Instead of heading straight for the rummaging in the living room, Tyler slipped through the kitchen's side door. His gun was still on the counter. Moving as fast as possible, Tyler circled the counter. Before he made it to his service weapon, huge arms encircled him, squeezing his arm to his sides and the air from his lungs. Tyler touched his chin to his chest, gathering momentum before throwing his head back and cracking his attacker across the bridge of his nose. He couldn't let this man win. Tyler's heartbeat pounded in his ears. Adrenaline raced through his veins. He dropped his weight, throwing the man off balance and breaking his hold. The moment he was free, Tyler grabbed the gun. An instant before he turned on his assailant, lights exploded behind his left eye half a second before the pain hit. Tyler didn't let the punch take him out. With the weight of his weapon filling his palm, Tyler's heart slowed. His training set in.

He pressed the gun to the man's head. "Hands where I can I see them."

Once the dude realized he was at gunpoint, his hands went up. Tyler slowly walked backward and hit the lights.

"Who the fuck are you?"

"That's my question," Tyler said, refusing to back down an inch.

"Brad," the guy said, looking pissed as hell. "This is my house."

"The fuck you say," Tyler said, but his mind reeled. This was Brad? Goddamn. No wonder Jace had a complex. Tyler thought he might be developing one too by just looking at the guy. He was huge. Tyler was six-two, and this dude towered over him.

His arms were massive. Those things had nothing on his face. He looked like a fucking model. The only thing saving Tyler's pride was the knowledge the man was ugly on the inside. Otherwise, those blue eyes would buy Brad anything. That was the kind of power that should only be used for good.

"It used to be my house," Brad argued, sounding annoyed and pulling Tyler back on topic.

"What the hell is going on out here?" Jace asked, sounding more tired than upset as he appeared at Tyler's side.

"Tell this fool to stop pointing his gun at me," Brad said, dropping his hands.

"Put your fucking hands up," Tyler repeated. He didn't give a fuck if this wasn't some stranger breaking in. He'd still shoot the fucker and not miss a single night's sleep. "This isn't a game. Breaking into someone's home is a crime."

"Jace doesn't care if I come in without knocking."

"Actually, I do," Jace said, but it was obvious Brad wasn't listening. He was too busy eating up the sight of Jace in nothing more than workout shorts. Tyler wanted to demand he go put some clothes on, but he had bigger problems at the moment.

"You also broke our window," Tyler reminded him. "That's destruction of property."

Brad's expression turned thunderous at Tyler's claim. "Jace's window. Not yours, and it was an accident. I couldn't see in the dark."

"It's Tyler's window too," Jace said, trying to be heard again.

"It's all right, baby. I got this."

Jace flashed him a smile. It slipped away as his gaze landed on Tyler's face. "What happened to your eye?" Without waiting for Tyler to answer, Jace gasped.

"Oh my God. Did he hit you? I'll kill him." Jace took two steps in Brad's direction before Tyler snagged him around the waist. As much as he'd like to let Jace fuck up Brad, he couldn't risk it.

"Don't worry, babe. He broke in here and assaulted a police officer. I'll make sure he gets the maximum sentence."

"Wait. What?" For the first time, Brad looked genuinely frightened, which had been Tyler's intention. He couldn't actually see to the man getting any amount of time. That was all up to the courts, but he enjoyed watching Brad squirm. "It wasn't like that," Brad argued. "Paige called, saying she was worried about Jace. He hasn't been returning her texts or answering her calls. She was worried something happened to you," Brad added, obviously hoping to appeal to Jace's good nature.

"So she called you?" Jace asked,

sounding odd—like a mixture of furious, hurt, and confused.

Tyler was good with letting Jace ask the questions. His mind was too busy thinking about how Paige had to go. Jace had been so right. They needed her out of their lives. He didn't doubt for a second that sending Brad had been a calculated move on her part. Unlike Jace, Tyler understood all Brad's motives for treating Jace as he had. Mostly, the guy was just a dick, but he also tried keeping Jace in his place, scared shitless he'd lose him. It was fucked up, but so was Brad.

Brad shrugged. "She knows, even though we're no longer together, I'd always take care of you."

Jace snorted. "Funny, all she ever says to me is how big of an ass you are." Jace rubbed the spot between his eyes, as if a headache bloomed there.

Brad's eyes stayed locked on Jace's

every move. "Is that a wedding band?" The man's question came out low, sounding hurt yet deadly.

Jace dropped his gaze to his hand. "Yes." His tone sounded conversational. Tyler bit his bottom lip to keep from laughing.

"Paige didn't tell me you remarried."

"That's because I didn't tell her," Jace said with a shrug.

"What?" Tyler snapped. It was his turn to get pissed.

At his open surprise, Brad snorted. "How could you marry this idiot?"

"This idiot has a gun pointed at your head," Tyler reminded him. "So, really, who's the dumbass in this equation?" Tyler asked, reaching his limit. He focused on Jace once more. "Why haven't you told anyone?" It hurt more than he imagined, realizing Jace was ashamed.

Jace's shoulders fell. "I've told

239

everyone who'll listen," Jace said, sounding proud and taking away some of the sting before adding, "Except Paige. You don't know how she can get. If I told her, I know exactly what she'd say. First, she'd tell me I'm crazy, and we just met." A sexy smile touched Jace's lips, carrying away the rest of Tyler's irritation. He fucking loved this man. "Then I'd try to explain how I knew you were the one the moment you showed up at my door, looking for Jimmy. I felt in my bones."

Brad snorted. "You felt it in one bone."

They ignored him. Tyler couldn't stop hanging on Jace's every word, and Jace had more to say. "Then Paige would try reminding me how this fool treated me," he said, tossing a careless wave in Brad's direction. "I'd argue how you treat me like a king—how you're nothing like him. But then, she'd try to convince me you're a cheat by pointing out how many hours you work and how often you have to stay gone. No matter what I try saying, she'll twist it and turn it ugly. We're not ugly. I couldn't listen to her while she tainted this," Jace said, motioning between them.

Because Jace was right, they were beautiful, he couldn't let Jace keep standing there in the middle of more of Paige's ugliness. "I've got you now, baby. Just go back to bed and let me take care of everything."

With a nod, Jace headed back down the hall. Brad's gaze ate up every move Jace made. Tyler almost felt sorry for the guy—almost.

With his gun still held on Brad, Tyler grabbed his cell phone and pretended to dial.

"What are you doing?" Brad asked as his attention snapped back to Tyler.

"Calling this in," Tyler said, keeping his voice nonchalant. "As I said, assaulting a police officer is serious business."

"Dude, I'm so sorry. I thought you were some strange guy in Jace's house. I thought he was in danger."

"Our house," Tyler reminded him.

"Yeah," Brad immediately agreed. "Y'alls' house. Look, I can't go to jail. I need my job. My mom depends on me to help with her bills and stuff. I thought I was helping out a friend. That's all."

The guy was a douche and Tyler still wanted to shoot him, but he'd been played by Paige just as Jace had been for years. Still, Tyler couldn't let this go without some comfort this wouldn't happen again. "If I let you walk away from here, you can't ever come back."

"Dude, I'm out. Jace has been done with me for a long time."

Tyler nodded. Damn straight Jace was done. "Would you be willing to give a statement against Paige, making it possible for us to file a restraining order against her?" Tyler wasn't playing. That bitch had to go.

"Yeah, anything."

An evil smile stretched Tyler's lips. "You down to scare the hell out of Paige?"

Brad's smile matched Tyler's. "Bitch has you pointing a gun at me. I'm in."

Tyler set his gun aside, freeing Brad. "Call Paige, tell her this is your one phone call, and you're using it let her know you've told the police everything. You've already agreed to testify against her for setting you up."

Brad snickered as he pulled out his cell phone.

Tyler stopped him. He held his phone out to Brad. "Use mine. She'll never believe it's your one phone call if she recognizes your number."

Brad snorted as he waved away Tyler's

offer. "Please. She's not that bright. I've got this."

Tyler watched in equal parts humor and horror as Brad convinced Paige the police were on their way right that second to get her. He'd never seen anyone more suited for an acting career. The guy was a natural born liar. He almost wished Jace was witnessing it as well, but Jace had already seen this man lie too many times over the years. Tyler's features hardened. He felt it happen. Never again, Tyler vowed. He would never allow people like this to invade Jace's life again. His man deserved a beautiful life. Tyler would make damn sure he got it.

*

Jace stared up at the darkened ceiling, trying not to think. Curiosity ate him alive, but he stayed put. Tyler would take care of everything. It was a good thing too. Every time Jace thought about Brad putting his hands on Tyler, he wanted to go back out there and unman him. No one hurt his man. If Tyler ended up with a black eye tomorrow, Jace might still decide to hunt that bastard down and make him pay. And Paige; he'd never been more fucking done with anyone in his life. Before Brad had shown up at his door, Jace had been on the fence about how to handle Paige. Now, fuck her. No one came between Jace and his husband.

Tyler reappeared in the doorway.

Jace's breath caught at the back of his throat. "I didn't hear any sirens."

"No," Tyler said with a shake of his head. "We came to an understanding."

Tyler had never looked sexier to Jace than he did in that moment. Jace didn't doubt for a second Tyler had done something badass to get Brad to agree to go away without a fight. Still.

"Was your agreement you wouldn't kill

him? Because I made no such promises."

"I don't want you anywhere near that guy."

Tyler's calmly spoken demand had Jace gripping the sheets to keep from touching himself. Dear God. The hot possessiveness in Tyler's tone set Jace on fire. He no longer cared what happened after he left Tyler alone with Brad.

Jace licked his suddenly parched lips and tempted fate. "What will you do if I disobey?"

Tyler pushed away from the doorframe and silently headed for the drawer filled with all their toys. Jace already knew what would happen next. His stomach quivered with anticipation.

"I think I should punish you now, before you get any ideas."

Jace bit his bottom lip to keep from whimpering. This was his life now. Tyler was everything. In a few days, they'd disappear and everything with Paige and Brad would be ancient history. The weight that had lived on Jace's shoulders for years was gone. For so long, he'd felt unworthy of anything. Now he enjoyed using his newfound confidence against Tyler.

He tossed back the covers and shifted his weight, making his abs harden. Just as he'd known Tyler would, the man eyed Jace from head to foot. Tyler palmed the erection tenting his boxers as if incapable of not touching himself by only the sight of Jace's nude body.

"You were in here naked with Brad down the hall."

It wasn't a question. Jace didn't respond. Instead, he boldly stroked his cock, taunting Tyler.

Tyler's eyes flashed with something dangerous. "I'm about to spank you," Tyler promised, making Jace's dick leak. "Then

I'll fuck you until you can't sit tomorrow. You'll never think of Brad again."

Jace hadn't thought of Brad since meeting Tyler, but if Tyler wanted to punish him, Jace would keep that bit of information to himself. After all, he did love the sting of Tyler's palm on his ass. Maybe tomorrow, Jace would tell Tyler all about how no one held a candle to him. There was no one else in Jace's head and there never would be again. Then again, maybe he'd drag this out. Jace could handle a lifetime of being chained to the bed as long as Tyler was the one who held the key.

Chapter 8

The knock landing on the front door had Adam staring at the slab of wood in open wonder. No one knew he was here. As far as everyone was concerned, the house had been empty since Jace and Tyler took off on their trip around the world. There also shouldn't be any deliveries. Jace and Tyler's mail now went to a P.O. box and Adam got all his mail in New York. Another loud knock landed against the wood. Adam moved closer. There was no soliciting in this neighborhood, so it couldn't be that.

"Do you plan on answering that?" Kano asked, dragging Adam from his musings.

With a shrug, Adam pulled the door open. Paige stood on the other side.

She squealed when she saw him, nearly piercing Adam's eardrums. "Oh my

God. You're home." She pulled him in for a hug. Adam let it happen while stamping down his surprise over her appearance. "How long are you here for?"

Adam stepped back and allowed Paige inside. "Um. Just until we get all this squared away."

Paige's gaze swept the room. Her expression turned puzzled as she eyed the bare walls and mounds of boxes before focusing on Kano. "I feel like I'm missing a lot. Who is your friend?"

Before Adam could respond, Kano took over the way he always did. "Kano Aramante, and you are?" He let the question hang in the air. It dripped with British disdain, sounding as if Paige was a stranger intruding on their time. Of course, nothing pissed Kano off like having a second of his time wasted.

"Paige Carpenter," Paige said, clutching her purse tighter, as if Kano couldn't be trusted. Since Kano was currently sporting a fifty-thousand-dollar suit, the move was beyond ridiculous. "What is a man of your... stature doing here—alone—with someone as sweet as Adam? I can't think Jace would appreciate that."

Adam bit the inside of his cheek hard. Paige had all but called Kano old and insinuated he was out to molest an innocent child. In truth, Kano was only thirty-seven, and Adam was no child.

Kano's icy gaze flashed in such a way Adam had come to know too well. The man was sharpening his claws and deciding in which way he would ruin this woman. To Adam's surprise, Kano didn't immediately attack. "I'm helping Adam pack."

Paige smirked.

Kano's steel-gray eyes narrowed. He didn't like Paige. Adam could feel it. That tidbit had Adam eyeing Paige with interest. Kano was never wrong about anyone.

Her evil smile didn't abate. "Dressed like that?" she asked, pointing out Kano's expensive suit compared to Adam's ragged jeans and worn out T-shirt.

Something wicked passed over Kano's features. Adam drew a slow breath through his nose. It was damn sexy when Kano turned condescending. "I don't have to get my hands dirty to help anyone do anything."

Judging by Paige's sneer, things were on the verge of turning ugly. Adam intervened. "Did you need something, Paige?"

She turned away from Kano, dismissing him. Adam couldn't resist checking Kano's reaction. No one ever dismissed him. The man's eyes flashed with humor, as if he found Paige to be a weak target.

"I came by to speak to Jace, but I wasn't expecting all this," she said, motioning toward the boxes. "Since we don't work together any longer, we don't speak as much as we used to. In fact, it's been so long, I've lost his number. You know how it is. I got a new phone and all my contacts didn't transfer. Is Jace moving?" she asked, eyeing the boxes once more.

Instead of answering, Adam dug his phone out. "I've got his number." He swiped the screen, scrolling through his contacts and searching for Jace's number.

Kano's hand covered Adam's phone, stopping the motion. Adam's head jerked up. Irritation ran through him. Kano's expression had Adam's hackles falling as quickly as they rose. He looked calculating.

"Jace hasn't been here since the day he called to tell his boss he wouldn't be

253

back. Even I know that, and I've never met the man."

Adam held in his snort. That was because Adam refused to let Kano meet Jace, but that was another story.

"It seems strange you'd show up here on the exact day someone is here. I'm not much on coincidences."

Kano had a point. It was odd. Paige's closed expression piqued Adam's curiosity even further. The woman did seem... off.

"I told Jace I would keep an eye on the place. As I was passing by, I saw a light on."

Adam shoved his phone in his back pocket. He didn't think it was such a good idea to give out Jace's number after all.

Kano confirmed his feelings. "Do you live in this neighborhood?" His tone said he knew she didn't.

Paige shifted from foot to foot. "No."

"So, you were driving by, through a

gated community, to check on a friend's house who even you admit you haven't spoken to in so long you no longer know how to contact them?"

Adam knew by the way Paige's shoulders squared, she wasn't backing down. "I don't know you. It's none of your concern what arrangement I have with my friend."

Kano's eyes took on a hard edge. Adam's knees weakened. The man transformed into the owner of the world's largest fashion magazine in front of Adam's eyes. This was the powerful version of Kano that Adam couldn't resist.

Kano pulled out his phone. "I would feel better if I spoke with my friend at the Justice Department before Adam hands out any personal information. As you pointed out, I don't know you. For all I know, Jace has a restraining order against you and you shouldn't even be here." Kano focused on Adam. "While I'm doing that, you should probably go ahead and call the police to be safe."

Adam's mouth fell open as Paige scrambled for the door. She scratched at the knob as if stuck in a horror film with a killer on her heels. Once she made it through the door, she was gone. Adam stared at the spot where she'd been standing while trying to process what happened.

A low chuckle caressed Adam's ears. Without thought, he pressed his hand to his stomach to stop the butterflies. Once he had his emotions under control, he met Kano's stare. Those steel eyes, damn. No amount of preparation could stop would they did to Adam.

"Do you really know someone at the Justice Department?"

Kano snorted. "Not only do I not know anyone, I'm not even certain what they do, but I recognize crazy from a mile away. Stalkers flock to me. That woman had 'nutter' stamped all over her."

Everyone and everything flocked to Kano, which was why Adam refused to be walked on. He would never be special to Kano. That traitorous thought kept sneaking its way in. As if he read Adam's thoughts and hoped to prove him wrong, Kano closed the distance between them. "Aren't you glad I ignored you when you told me not to come here?"

Adam licked his lips. The way Kano stared at his mouth had Adam scared he'd give Kano everything if the man pressed. All Adam had was his pride. "No. As always, I would've been fine without you."

A low laugh left Kano's perfect lips. It left Adam paralyzed as Kano's hand cupped his cheek. Kano's thumb brushed Adam's bottom lip. Dang. He was so screwed. No matter how hard he tried,

Adam couldn't move. All he could do was eat Kano's beautiful face alive with his stare.

"I don't need your permission to protect you, Adam. I always take care of what's mine."

Keep an eye out for Adam's book, Unmask. (http://mybook.to/Unmask)

Author note: Since Adam has been off living his life in New York, his story's timeline will run concurrent with this story.

About the Author

Charity Parkerson is an award winning and multi-published author with several companies. Born with no filter from her brain to her mouth, she decided to take this odd quirk and insert it in her characters.

*2015 Readers' Favorite Award Winner
*Winner of 2, 2014 Readers' Favorite Awards
*2015 Passionate Plume Award Finalist
*2013 Readers' Favorite Award Winner
*2013 Reviewers' Choice Award Winner
*2012 ARRA Finalist for Favorite Paranormal Romance
*Five-time winner of The Mistress of the Darkpath

Connect with her online:

--Join my street team:
facebook.com/TeamCharityParkerson

--Sign up for my newsletter:
http://bit.ly/CharityNews
--Website: charityparkerson.com
--Facebook:
facebook.com/authorCharityParkerson
facebook.com/TheMenofSin

--Twitter: twitter.com/CharityParkerso